Joseph R Gorrell

Sins Absolved

A Romance

Joseph R Gorrell

Sins Absolved
A Romance

ISBN/EAN: 9783337347840

Printed in Europe, USA, Canada, Australia, Japan

Cover: Foto ©Andreas Hilbeck / pixelio.de

More available books at **www.hansebooks.com**

SINS ABSOLVED;

A ROMANCE.

War, Religion and Love.

BY

DR. J. R. GORRELL.

DES MOINES:
THE KENYON PRINTING & MFG. CO.
1895.

DEDICATION:

*To the remaining soldiers of Iowa, Ohio, Indiana, and
Minnesota, who are familiar with many of the
facts in " Sins Absolved," this book is
respectfully dedicated.*

NEWTON, IOWA, DECEMBER 1, 1895.

CONTENTS.

SINS ABSOLVED.

CHAPTER I.

THE FIRES KINDLED.

"Twelve o'clock! Why, Agnes, I did not know it was so late: I think an apology is due you for overstepping the bounds of propriety, as I have done to-night. Give me your hand in token that my offense shall not be remembered against me."

"Oh, certainly," she said, giving him her hand, "I am the most forgiving of mortals, and I solemnly pronounce your 'sin absolved.'" Then, with an expression of deep tenderness in her soft gray eyes, in lower tones continued: "Donald, I trust you will never again think of apologizing for staying too long with me. I have been happy to-night; I am always happy when you are with me."

The unexpected reply thrilled the soul of Donald Wallace like an electric shock, and for the first time in his life he felt the fervent rays of the dawn of an unknown emotion. Not a word was spoken of love: a love that was to bring to both so much sorrow and so much happiness. He merely said, "Agnes, I thank you. Good-night."

Donald Wallace and Agnes Murray were both of Scottish ancestry. Their parents, in whose veins flowed the blood of some of Scotland's bravest and noblest men, came from the Highlands of that country to this at an early date. Having been friends and neighbors in their native land, they bought residences adjoining each other in a flourishing Puritan village in Massachusetts.

Donald and Agnes were their only children, and, being possessed of ample wealth, no expense was spared in their culture. Private teachers, the best that money could procure, gave them instructions together at Agnes' home. They were, therefore, playmates and schoolmates, but appeared more like brother and sister than members of different families. Donald was two years older than Agnes, and was at all times her superior in scholarship. He graduated at Harvard College at the age of eighteen, with the highest honors. After his graduation he spent four years in the best colleges in Europe. He enjoyed the personal acquaintance of Max Muller, Herbert Spenser, and the venerable Humboldt. After the completion of his college course in Europe, he spent two years traveling in the Orient, where he became familiar with the languages, the customs, the legends and the theological learning of Budha, Brahma, and Confucius.

In personal appearance, on his return to his native land, which occurred on the first day of February, 1861, he presented the appearance of an athlete and

scholar. He stood six feet in his stock-
ings, was broad shouldered and full
chested : his massive head and his large.
blue eyes were not forgotten after having been seen. He was reserved and
refined in his demeanor. The Scotch
strength of character was apparent in
every word and action.

Agnes Murray was at this time a trifle
above medium size. with a physique as
perfect as that of Venus. Her Grecian
face combined sweetness and true womanly dignity. Her native modesty,
superadded to the highest culture attain-
able in the institutions of learning that
admitted women, and two years of instruction in music by the best teachers
in Italy. gave to her a charming personality. and a womanly grace not often
possessed by anyone. at that time.

It was Donald's intention. after a few
months' rest. to enter the legal profession. During the two months after his
return from Europe he spent many

evenings in Agnes' company at her father's home. It was on the evening of April 11, 1861, that for some reason, unknown to himself, he had tarried longer than usual, which necessitated the apology at the beginning of this chapter.

On the day of the 12th the thrilling news flashed over the wires that Fort Sumter had been fired on. The whole neighborhood was aroused; no subject was mentioned but war; even on that day there were trembling lips and tear-bedimmed eyes; enlistment was on every hand the subject under consideration.

Late in the afternoon Donald rode rapidly to the Murray mansion, and was met at the gate by Agnes. As he dismounted he gave her his hand, to which she clung as she had never done before. "Agnes," he said, "as soon as I heard Fort Sumter had been fired on, and I had determined to raise a company and enter the service, something said to me,

'Go and see Agnes,' and I am here. I suppose I am here to have you urge me to raise a company quickly, enter the service. and if need be, give my life a willing sacrifice to my country."

She still held his hand. and with a quiver of her lips which she could not conceal, said : "I can't urge you. I know you will do your duty, and whatever that may be, I shall always feel a deep interest in your welfare."

They lingered for an hour at the gate, and then walked slowly and thoughtfully to the house.

He said, when taking Mr. Murray's hand, "I have found it somewhat difficult to make up my mind, but I have reached a conclusion and shall act at once. I shall call a meeting at the court house to-morrow night and ask for volunteers. Any aid you can give me in publishing a notice of the meeting will be appreciated. I am now ready to say good-bye."

Mr. and Mrs. Murray gave him an affectionate farewell without emotion, but Agnes' hand trembled and her eyes filled with tears as she said, "May Heaven bless and protect you."

He hurried to the gate, mounted his horse and rode away.

The meeting at the court house was more than a success. The fires of patriotism were already burning in every home and the whole people were aroused. The court house was filled to its maximum capacity. Donald spoke for an hour, surprising all with his deep earnestness, his patriotism, and his thrilling eloquence. He began calmly, in a tone that was hardly above a whisper, but as he proceeded the whole man was gradually absorbed and transfigured, as in a fountain of fire, which then poured forth in one tumultuous and overwhelming torrent of melody, the splendor of appeal, of pathos, and invective, and sarcasm, and beauty, till those present lost

consciousness of self, and were borne
away as on a "golden river flowing to the
lands of dreams." His eloquence had
in it the affluent potentiality of the ris-
ing sun : of the lonely mountain : of the
long successive surges of the resounding sea. His periods were as lucid as
the light; his logic was irresistible:
"his words were crystal clear;" his
magnificent person towered in dignity,
and seemed colossal in its imperial
grandeur; his voice grew in volume as
he became more aroused, and his language glowing with the fire of conviction, rose and swelled, and broke like
the great ocean wave that shakes the
rock-bound shore. His speech was ad-
dressed to the reason, and not to the
imagination, but you seemed to feel the
rush of the tempest, and to hear the
crash of breakers and the howling of
frantic gales and sobbing wail of homeless winds "in the bleak and haunted
regions of perpetual night." Several

times he brought the entire audience to their feet, and when he reached the climax — the duty of the American citizen in the hour of his country's peril — the wildest excitement prevailed.

At the close of his address volunteers were called for, and Donald's name headed the list. Within thirty minutes the necessary number of names were added to fill the company. and Donald Wallace was elected captain by acclamation. A telegram was sent to the governor tendering him the company, and his acceptance was received before the expiration of an hour. A second telegram from the governor to Captain Wallace, furnishing transportation for his company, and directing him to report at rendezvous with his company at the earliest possible moment, was received in a few moments after the first. Captain Wallace directed all those who had enlisted to meet him at the depot the next morning at 11 o'clock, as the train left at 11 :30.

The morning came, and with it a large and enthusiastic crowd of people. Everybody wanted to see the first company leave for the seat of war. The old and the young, the infirm and the strong, men, women and children, many of them having arrived before sunrise.

And such scenes; such joys and sorrows; such mingled emotions of hope and fear, of partings and of blessings. Aged parents parting with only sons, mothers' last farewells, and the deep suppressed sob of lovers, gave emotions before unknown to me, and reminded me of the final judgment, when loved ones are to be separated forever, if orthodoxy proves to be the religion of Jesus Christ.

In less than ten days the requisite number of companies had arrived at the regimental rendezvous. The regiment was organized and Capt. Donald Wallace of Company A was elected major. In a few days after the regimental organization was completed, it was ordered to the front, and box-cars transported the precious freight. Less than thirty-three per cent ever returned. Sixty per cent of as noble young men as ever died on the battle-field were buried among strangers.

The life of the soldier now begins in earnest. The regiment goes into camp within twenty miles of a Confederate force of superior number.

While in this camp and before they had been in an engagement the following letter came to Major Wallace:

NEW YORK, April —, 1861.

MAJOR WALLACE :

My Dear Friend,— You will probably be surprised to receive a letter from me, as you did not ask me to write to you. I have determined to spend a short time with my relatives in Scotland. Why I go I will explain to you if we ever meet again. I leave New York on the earliest steamer bound for London. I will write to you again as soon as I reach my destination, and give you my address. I have no right to ask you to write to me, but as I once felt justified in saying to you, " I shall always feel a deep interest in your welfare," it appears to me not improper to let you know just what I said, and that I meant it then, and I mean it now.   Your friend,

AGNES MURRAY.

CHAPTER II.

DICK DALE.

The routine duties of camp life had continued less than ten days. The colonel, lieutenant-colonel, the major and the adjutant were at dinner, when the colonel remarked:

"I saw in a New York paper this morning that a large ocean steamer had been wrecked in a storm at sea and all on board were lost except three persons. A young fearless fellow whose name was Dick Dale was one of the survivors. I remember his name for the reason that I knew his father. Dick, the captain, and the first mate only were saved. They were the last to leave the vessel in a lifeboat, and they alone were picked up. Dick, like his father, was a man of remarkable coolness in danger, and personal courage far up toward the border line of reckless-

ness, and he behaved like an old seaman.
It became apparent to the crew in a few
moments after the storm of great violence
struck her that she could not survive,
and the passengers became wild with
fear, and in defiance of the orders of the
captain and the earnest protestations of
Dick Dale they launched the lifeboats
and hurried into them, in a sea in which no
lifeboat could live. By the way, Major, a
favorite among the passengers, described
as a sweet-faced, sad-hearted girl, though
a special effort was made to save her, was
lost. Her name was Agnes Murray, and
her home was where you enlisted from.
I suppose you were not acquainted with
her?"

The major stared wildly at the colonel,
his face grew deadly pale and his voice
trembled as he said, "Have you the
paper?"

It was apparent to the mess that some
awful emotion stirred his soul. The
colonel rose in dignified silence, brought

the paper and handed it to him. The
major left the table and went to his tent.

The account of the storm and its
results were as follows : "Great storm at
sea : the steamer L——, believed to be one
of the safest ocean vessels, is lost and all
on board lost, except three persons. A
gale of great fury struck her at 7 :30 A. M. ;
many of the passengers were in bed :
the signal of danger was given and the
wildest excitement prevailed. The lifeboats were torn from their places,
launched and filled with excited passengers, only to be swallowed up by an
angry sea. The boats were launched in
defiance of the captain's orders, whose
strong, firm voice rose above the roar of
the storm, 'No boat can live in such a
sea.' One of the passengers, whose
name was Dick Dale displayed the courage of a true hero; he declined to go
into the lifeboat while there were others
on board who were more anxious to live
than he was. He walked quietly among

the passengers and urged them to be
calm, with a coolness that surprised even
the captain. The only female passenger
who exhibited neither fear or excitement.
was Miss Agnes Murray. Twice before
she consented to go into the lifeboat she
had declined, saying, 'It's no matter
about me.' When all had left the vessel and the relentless billows of a wild and
boisterous ocean had swallowed them, the
captain, the first mate, and Dick Dale
stepped into the only remaining and least
seaworthy lifeboat, just as the vessel
sunk. They were picked up six hours
later by a vessel bound for New York."

What the major's emotions were as he
read the account no one will ever know.
An hour later he sent a note to the colonel,
asking to be excused from duty for two
days. He did not go to supper that
evening, nor to breakfast or dinner the
next day. At 2 o'clock the colonel in
person went hurriedly to the major's
tent, and said, "Scouts have just come

in and they have informed me that
Humphrey Marshall is coming down
Middle Creek with a force of twice our
number, and we shall have to fight within
an hour or retreat, and I came to ask you
if you wished to be excused from duty."

Wallace sprang to his feet with the
bound of an athlete and exclaimed, "*Excused from duty!* No, Colonel, I shall
be ready for business in three minutes."

The whole man was in an instant transformed from a dejected, heart-broken
fellow to a man of the most soldierly
bearing I ever saw.

"Colonel," said Major Wallace, "let
us meet him, and if it is to our advan-
tage, let us choose our battle-field, as
Wellington did at Waterloo."

The long roll was sounded and in ten
minutes the regiment was marching up
Middle Creek to meet the enemy. It is
probably not an exaggeration to say,
that no officer during the war presented
a finer or more soldierly appearance than

did Major Wallace that day. His massive and finely proportioned physique, his faultless dress, and his magnificent plume made him a conspicuous mark. He was happy almost to hilarity.

They had marched less than half an hour until Confederate cavalry was in their front. The regiment was halted for a few minutes and a council of war held between the colonel, lieutenant-colonel and the major.

The major said, " Colonel, I am familiar with this whole neighborhood. I can take 300 men, go up this ravine, cross that low spur of the mountain, and in thirty minutes can have my men partially concealed, and be in position to deal a destructive blow when they least expect it. I hope you will excuse me for this suggestion, and I am at your service."

The colonel took his hand and said, " Major, I thank you. Make your selection and proceed at once."

3

Within five minutes the major and 300 picked men disappeared up the ravine.

"The point at which I hope to make an attack," said Wallace, before leaving, "is less than half a mile distant, and I know at the first gun you will come to my assistance."

The colonel made his first speech to the remaining 700; he explained the danger in which their comrades were placed, and the necessity for prompt action at the signal of firing in their front. "This will be your first engagement, but I expect from you the coolness of veterans. Every man can cover himself with glory or disgrace. Less than heroic duty on our part will result in the same fate for the gallant Wallace and his noble three hundred, as came to Leonides at the pass of Thermopylæ, and they will go down as did the Spartans."

The speech was scarcely ended until the roll of musketry was heard and quickly followed by the thunder of a

battery. The major had not succeeded
in getting his men in just the position he
desired. As he reached the summit of
the low range of mountains his keen eye
observed a force of more than twice his
number less than 400 yards distant
already in line of battle supported by a
battery of six guns, and the advancing
Confederate skirmish line opened fire at
once. Every man grasped the situation.
The battery opened with grape and canister. The major saw the moment was
fearfully critical, and with his sword
flashing in the sunlight, his eye blazing
like that of Napoleon's at Austerlitz, he
dashed the whole length of the line in an
instant and shouted in a voice that
echoed from hill-top to hill-top and
sounded like distant thunder. "*That
battery must be taken. Courage, boys,
charge!*"

And such a charge; with the fearless-
ness of Roman soldiers they rushed to
victory or death; such relentless fury;

the courage of despair seized every man;
the line was rapidly decimated by volley
after volley of grape and canister at
short range: the line for an instant
wavers; the major re-forms them in an
instant; his horse is shot under him;
his orderly falls dead by his side; the
color-sergeant is mortally wounded: still
undaunted he bade them charge; fear
was banished, pity was forgotten: like a
cyclone they swept forward, leaving
death and destruction in their track. No
human beings could stand such a charge:
the gunners were killed at their posts;
the infantry fled; the victory was complete,—but at what a cost. Of the 300
who entered the engagement one-third
were gone. The colonel and the 700
made every effort in their power to reach
the battle-field, but they were too late.
It was fought and won before they
arrived.

The next morning after the battle a
young man came into camp and asked

for Major Wallace. He was directed to
the major's tent.

The major and the colonel were sitting
in front talking of their victory and of
the casualties of the day before.

The young man saluted them and said,
" I am Dick Dale ; I am one of the survivors of the ill-fated steamer L—, and I
would like to join your regiment if you
have a place for me."

The colonel took his hand and said,
" My dear fellow if you have the coolness
and courage of your father we need you,
we made a place for you yesterday :"
and he added sorrowfully as he walked
away, " You need an orderly, Major, as
yours was killed ; better give the boy a
trial."

The major and Dick went into the
tent and were seated. A painful silence
followed, neither one knowing how to
begin a conversation that both expected
would bring heart-sobs to one and perhaps to both.

At last before a word was spoken Dick took from his pocket a locket and handed it to the major, saying, "Miss Agnes Murray gave it to me and requested that if she was lost to give it to you, 'and you may say to him,' she said, 'my last thoughts were of him. If I survive return it to me.'"

The major opened it with trembling hands pressed it to his lips and sobbed aloud as if his heart would break. "O, Agnes! If I had told you what you were to me you would not have gone."

After a long silence, and he had somewhat regained his composure, he said, "Was she afraid to die?"

"I saw no evidence of fear. She and I were together on the deck when the storm struck us. We were discussing the threatening appearance: the thick black clouds, vivid lightning and terrific thunder and the apparent anxiety of the sailors gave us apprehensions of danger. Suddenly the fury of a storm at sea was upon us. The engine was disabled and the wheels stopped, and the great ocean steamer seemed to drop a hundred feet into a trough, the waves rose far above us on either side and we were helpless in midocean. The vessel was swept with waves and we would probably have been carried overboard, but for our firm hold on the railing. It was then she took the locket from her neck and gave it to me with the request already referred to. She also said with absolute indifference, as far as I could see, 'As to danger, you are an expert swimmer and your apparel being less cumbrous than mine you will probably be saved and I lost.' At that time the wildest excitement prevailed, and consternation seemed to be in every heart. The lifeboats were torn from their fastenings and launched wholly without judgment and in defiance to the orders of the captain. The captain said she left the - steamer in the third lifeboat before the

one in which I left. She was one of
twelve, he said, and before their boat was
ten feet away it capsized and the angels
came and took her. She was not afraid
to die, and I think she did not care to
live."

Dick rose and left the tent. The
major was in his place on dress parade
that evening, as if no forest fire had so
lately swept his soul, leaving desolation
in its track.

The next morning when the orderly
came for instructions, the major said,
"Dick, what is the matter, you are not
yourself this morning?"

"No, major, I am not: I cried all last
night. I fear I am not doing my duty.
I have a secret which would probably
make you more happy than you are, but
if I tell you, it will certainly make me
miserable: what shall I do?"

"Don't tell me unless I am mortally
wounded. I will not commit suicide by
purposely putting myself in danger, but

I will not step out of the way of a bullet to save my life. I will be killed within a year and then I will meet Agnes in heaven, and there will be no more heartaches for either of us. Don't cry any more, Dick, it's unsoldierly," and the tears came into his own eyes.

" Good-morning, Major," called the chaplain from the door of the tent.

" Come in, Chaplain."

" No, thank you; I merely called to ask you to announce on dress parade this evening that there will be preaching at 11 o'clock next Sunday from the colonel's tent."

" All right, Chaplain, I will do so with pleasure."

At the appointed time, the chaplain preached a typical orthodox sermon from the text: " The potter hath power over clay to make one vessel unto honor and another unto dishonor," interspersed with lengthy quotations from the Presbyterian confession of faith, teaching that a large per cent of the human family are doomed to an everlasting hell, without any reference to what their lives had been, but because of a decree that was purely arbitrary, and that a small number were "elected" to the glories of heaven without reference to "faith or the good works on the part of the creature," all for the glory of His justice and His mercy. He cited as evidence of the wrath of God the confusion of tongues at the tower of Babel, Sodom and Gomorrah and the salted fate of Lot's wife; the standing still of the sun for Joshua, and the cause of the miraculous interference of the laws of nature; the fall of man and the expulsion from the garden of Eden, and God's treatment of Job, all of which had a literal signification. Linked unto it was the sad hope that the brave comrades who had fallen a few days ago in defense of their flag, their country and their God, had been "elected," and

closed with the astounding statement,
that duty done was no guarantee of the
necessary fitness for the celestial sphere,
and that the statement in the Bible,
"Well done, good and faithful servants," must be restricted in its signification ; that it could only refer to those
having been elected before the foundations of the world were laid.

The next day the chaplain called on
the major and said, "I observed that
you paid close attention to the sermon
yesterday. Are you a church member ?"

"No, chaplain, I am not, but I had a
Christian mother ; she was the noblest
Unitarian I ever knew."

"I deeply regret, Major," said the
chaplain, "that your mind was so early
poisoned with the inconsistency of het-
erodoxy. As good a man as you are
ought to be a member of the Presbyterian church. The Unitarian church
denies the essential Godship of Jesus

and the literal translation of many other passages in the Bible; its influence is. therefore, in favor of irreligion."

" Mr. Chaplain. your premises appear to me defective, your reasoning fallacious and your conclusions erroneous. The human mind is naturally religious, and only rebels against that which appears unreasonable. Thinkers draw the line between those higher facts of consciousness. which transcend any exercise of the faculties we now possess. and that are likely ever to lie concealed in the unexplored labyrinthian jungles of the human soul. and of the alleged facts that are beginning to be recognized to be in defiance of human reason. You seem to forget that the thinking leaders in theology have begun to accept the conclusions of science, and have given a liberal and rationalistic explanation to the myth and legend of many statements in the Bible. Now, has any harm been done to the Bible? On the

contrary, it has been made all the more
precious to us by these new divine rev-
elations through science. From these
myths and legends, caught from earlier
civilization, we see an evolution of the
most important moral and religious truths
for our race. Religion has thus been liberated from the thralldom of theories
which thinking men saw could no longer
be maintained. Where is the irreligion
in the knowledge of the fact that the
accounts of creation, and of many other
earlier events in the sacred books, were
remembrances of lore obtained from the
Chaldeans? The beautiful story of
Joseph is derived from the Egyptian
romance, of which the hieroglyphics
may still be seen. The story of David
and Goliath is poetry. And Samp-
son, like so many other men of strength
in other religions, 'is probably a sun
myth.' What evil will result if it is
known that the inculcation of high duty
in the childhood of the world was em-

bodied in such quaint stories as those
of Jonah. Balaam and Lot? And what
is the harm in having learned that the
blessed founder of our religion *was a
man?* What matter if those who in-
corporated the creation lore of Baby-
lonia and other oriental nations in the
sacred book of the Hebrews mixed it
with their own conceptions and deduc-
tions? What evil is to come from the
fact that Darwin changed the whole
aspect of our creation myths: that
Lyell and his compeers placed the Hebrew story of the creation and of the
deluge of Noah among legends: that
Capernicus put an end to the literal
acceptance of the sun standing still
for Joshua; or that Halley, in pro-
mulgating his law of comets, put an
end to the doctrine of signs and wonders; that Pinel, in showing that all
insanity is physical disease, relegated
to the realm of mythology the witch of
Endor and all stories of demoniacal

possession; that the Rev. Dr. Shaff and
a multitude of recent Christian travelers
in Palestine have put into the realm of
legend the story of Lot's wife transformed into a pillar of salt; and that
anthropologists, by showing how man
has arisen everywhere from low, brutal
beginnings, have destroyed the whole
theological theory of the 'Fall of man.'
The great body of sacred literature
becomes more valuable to us, as we
grasp the law of evolution, that through
myth, parable and poem we are approaching a reasonable religion, taught
by Jesus Christ. Unitarianism is the
crystallization of the teaching of the
man of Galilee, with a full recognition
of the *eternal fact* that the laws of nature have never been interfered with,
and that a personal exemplification of
His teaching, which we believe to be
not only possible but the sensible thing
to do, *is life in Christ.*"

CHAPTER III.

HUGGING A DELUSION.

The routine of camp life continued for several months with but little to interrupt its monotony. Their communication with the base of supplies was occasionally cut off, necessitating foraging. Dick Dale soon established and maintained the reputation of a reckless forager and his daring several times came near costing him his life. On one occasion he left the camp early in the morning, expecting to return in time for dinner. One, two, three, four and five o'clock came and he had not returned. General anxiety was felt for his safety. The major had his horse saddled, his carbines and his revolvers in their places and his horse standing at his tent. For the first time in his soldier life he appeared nervous. His field glass had

been to his eye for an hour, looking in
every direction. Suddenly he dropped
his glass, mounted his horse, plunged
his spurs deep into his sides and was off
like the wind. Less than half a mile
brought him in full view of Dick closely
pursued by four mounted Confederates.
Dick's horse, though the best in the
regiment, impeded as he was by two
turkeys and seven chickens, was not a
match for the Kentucky thoroughbreds.
Instantly the major was by his side and
as he approached, pitched him a carbine,
and the next moment two of the Confederate saddles were empty and the
other two pursuers fled. Dick remarked
to the major, with a twinkle in his eye,
as they rode back to camp, each leading
a horse, "I don't know what I am to do
for feed for *two* horses; I have had to
divide my rations with one for the last
ten days."

On the following day, the colonel's
health being poor, he tendered his resig-

4

nation. The lieutenant-colonel was a man of remarkable modesty, and he requested that Major Wallace be commissioned colonel.

The major had steadily grown in the estimation of the men. His uniform kindness to them, his courage, and his persistent unwillingness to receive the best of that which was brought in by the foragers, and his dignified soldierly bearing was their ideal of a military hero, and they almost worshiped him.

In a few days after he was commissioned colonel he received marching orders, and in less than a month they were under fire more than thirteen hours in one of the bloodiest battles of the late war, which lasted two days.

Early in the battle the brigade commander to which his regiment belonged, was killed, and he being the ranking colonel at once took command of the brigade. He had two horses shot under him, and was shot through the calf of the leg, but remained at his post of duty under fire until the victory was won. He was brevetted brigadier-general "for unsurpassed gallantry on the battle-field." He remained on his horse and under heavy fire for six hours after he was wounded.

Twice a superior officer said to him. "The rear is the place for a wounded man, and while your country needs you right now, I fear you will faint from the loss of blood."

The colonel said. "I must be with my brigade when the final charge is made," *and he was.*

"My dear General," said the chaplain, " I am glad your wound is no worse, you will be in the saddle in a few days, but as you are a man of great personal courage and expose yourself to shot and shell that is sometimes believed to be needless, it appears to me to be a proper time for you to seek salvation through the blood of Jesus Christ. A vicarious atonement is needed by all, and those of a pure life are prone to be self-righteous and therefore need it more even than those having led a wicked life."

"The *blood of Jesus!*" exclaimed the general. "Well, Chaplain, I am not a coward on the battle-field, and I am not afraid of my record. As I am now in the hospital, surrounded by soldiers suffering with gangrene, and though my wound is slight it may be attacked with gangrene and I be mustered out to appear before the bar of God in a few hours, it is neither immodest nor bombastic in me to say what I believe to be the truth of myself."

"Hello, Dick: here you are again. I suppose you are going to dress that leg. Mr. Chaplain come again. I want to have a longer conversation with you upon the subject under discussion to-day."

"Dick sit down on the edge of the bed near me; I want to talk to you. I like the surgeon; he is a jolly, whole-soul, good fellow, and he is very kind to me, but I do think your touch is lighter than his, and I know you pull the lint out of that rat hole in my leg with less pain than he does. I don't know what I would do if it was not for you. I think you would steal the Southern Confederacy blind to get me something to eat. But, Dick, you are a bold, reckless fellow; you take chances that are not demanded by the highest soldierly bearing. I was watching you when you carried that box of cartridges through that awful storm of minie-balls. sweetened with grape and canister, and I saw your horse fall. A shudder came over me and I said to a corps commander who was near by me, 'My God! Our best orderly is killed.' We saw you spring to your feet, grab the cartridges, and on the dead run, take them to the captain through a storm of lead and fire from which we saw no hope of escape. He directed me to put you in the line of promotion, and he brevetted you major

for gallantry on the battle-field. By the
way, Dick, do you know that if you had
been killed when your horse was shot
under you the battle would have been
lost, and the whole country would to-day
be in mourning over the defeat, instead
of rejoicing as it now is over a great
victory, and defeat in that battle would
have prolonged the war at a cost of
millions of money, and thousands of
lives."

"Why, General," said Dick, "what
have I done that you should slap me in
the face with such scathing irony? nobody but you pays any attention to me:
they say I am proud because I am your
orderly. I am scarcely spoken to once
a day, and no one comes to my tent. I
might as well be in a great wilderness as
here. Just yesterday the cook called me
a damned stuck-up dude, because I
couldn't bring him a pail of water when
I was coming to dress your leg, and
when I told what I was going to do, he

said, ' Oh, hell; you dress his leg, that's
too damned thin : let the surgeon do that,
and you bring me a pail of water, or I
will put a head on you.' I never heard
such language in all my life ; it frightened me: And now if you turn against
me I will go home."

"Well, Dick, in the first place, you
have no home ; in the second place you
are an enlisted man and can't go home ;
in the third place you are the best orderly
in the army, and in the fourth place I
meant just what I said, and there was
no irony in it. When you came back
to me after delivering the cartridges,
I felt then as I do now, that I would
like to embrace you as Napoleon did
Marshal Ney."

"Well, General, as you are in earnest,
you have my permission ; for, if I could
be hugged into the delusion, for a few
moments even, that I was like Marshal
Ney, I would be happy. Even that
would beat no hugging, and I have ob-

served that in army life there is a great
dearth of that kind of entertainment."

"Yes, Dick; you, my orderly, was,
in the providence of God, the cause of
the great victory, and you prevented
defeat. I do not mean a special providence, for that would mean a *changeable
deity*, a special adjustment of something that had not been anticipated and
provided for, and that was not in the
original plan, but I mean in the grand
sweep of God's plans you were the key-
stone in the arch. You know the last
desperate charge of the enemy, that was
so magnificently repulsed by our brigade, occurred within ten minutes after
that company got the cartridges from
your hands. You also know that the
company was out of ammunition, and
that it was in almost the mathematical
center of the brigade. And you know
that brigade held the post of honor, and
of the greatest danger in the line of
battle. You know our whole line was

advanced, and the final charge all along
the line, that resulted in rout and victory, occurred twenty-three minutes
thereafter. If that company had given
way at that awfully critical moment, as
they would have done in five minutes,
what then? For no amount of valor
will hold men in line without ammunition. Even Roman soldiers or Napoleon's old guard would not attempt to
repel a charge without means of defense. Not even the invincible Grecian
phalanx, commanded by Alexander the
Great, could have withstood such a
charge as that without the necessary
weapons of war."

"Dick. I like you for your kindness
to me, for your courage, and for your
unvarying dignified bearing. I have
observed your every action since you
came to the regiment from that awful
wreck at sea, in which all that was dear
to me went down, and no time, in
camp, on the march, or on the battle-

field, have you done anything except
that which would be commended if
done by the most scholarly Christian
gentleman; and more than that, Dick,"
and something came into his throat and
tears came into his eyes. "if my poor
lost Agnes had ever had a brother, I
would think you were he, you are so
much like her. Excuse my emotion,
Dick, and you must not cry; we are
soldiers now, and we are not supposed
to have hearts."

"General," said Dick. "I am only a
poor outcast. I have neither friends
nor home. I have nothing out of the
army to live for. The only person I
ever loved I then supposed did not return my love. I was saved from death
at sea, at the time of that wreck, almost
against my will, and I determined
to go into the army, and, if necessary,
throw my life away in battle. All I
can now do is to thank you, and to
assure you that I will prove worthy of

your respect and confidence if I have
to die to do it. I said, when you appointed me your orderly, that I would
perform all duties imposed upon me in a
fearless manner."

"Yes, my dear boy, and you have
more than kept your promise. But,
Dick, what have you to say about the
major's commission?"

"I would gladly accept it, and I
would not bring dishonor upon the
shoulder-straps. You will, however,
lose an orderly."

"But I will get a major for my staff,"
said the general.

"Hello! there comes the chaplain. You
may remain, Dick, and hear the conversation. I am going to do my utmost to
drive him into an impenetrable theological jungle, and then I am going to hammer
the brush. After all, the best man is
merely the product of ancestral influence
and his environment, and, if it be true
that humanity as a whole is to the stream

of creative energy as is a bubble on the surface of a river out of which it but recently came, and into which it is soon to go, even then a pure life pays an annual dividend of fifty per cent on the investment."

CHAPTER IV.

GENERAL WALLACE AND THE CHAPLAIN.

"Good-morning, General," said the chaplain, "will you have a cigar?"

"No, thank you, Chaplain, I never smoke. When we last parted, Mr. Chaplain, I had just said, in view of my present surroundings, it was neither immodest nor bombastic in me to say the truth, and that I am not afraid of my record. And you had said, 'No matter what my record had been, that I must obtain salvation through the blood of Jesus, in a vicarious atonement, or be doomed to endless perdition.' A personal reference to myself is, therefore, proper under the circumstances."

"Yes, General," said the chaplain, "I have been informed that your life has been exceptionally free from vice; that

you never gave your parents a moment's
unhappiness; that you were always obed-
ient; that you were at all times kind to
your playmates, and that you never stood
less than 100 in deportment in school or
in college; that you never used tobacco
in any form; that you never drank a drop
of spirituous liquors; that you never told
a falsehood; that you never have sworn
an oath; that your association with
women has been of a character that it
would not bring a blush to your mother's
cheek, nor to your own, if she had seen it
all; that you never declined to give lib-
erally to the needy, and that you exemplified in your daily life your belief in
the brotherhood of man and the father-
hood of God. The only accusation I ever
heard against you was, that you were
proud of your ancestry."

"Well, Mr. Chaplain," said Wallace,
"that appears to me to be overdrawn;
if you are not mistaken it is strange that
I did not die young. What I was about

to say of myself was that I have never
for one hour forgotten the pale angelic
face of my dying mother. I was fifteen
years old. As the death dew gathered
on her brow she beckoned me to come
to her. As I knelt by her bed, she put
her hand on my head and said, 'Donald, I gave you to God before you were
born, and I have given you to him every
day since, and I know he accepted you.
Continue to do your duty fearless of
consequences, and you will meet me in
heaven,' and her sweet soul passing
away, was received by angel hands and
welcomed by angelic hearts to a home in
heaven. My mother, in my early childhood, taught me this poem, and there
have been but few days in my life that I
have not repeated it, and it has been the
mainspring in my conduct:

"Courage, brother, do not stumble,
  Though the path be dark as night,
There is a star to guide the humble:
  Trust to God and do the right.

Perish policy and cunning,
  Perish all that fears the light,
Whether losing, whether winning,
  Trust to God and do the right.

There are those who need our helping,
  Those who listen for our song,
Only those who have been tortured,
  Know the bitterness of wrong.

So my heart will gladly help them
  Bear their burdens, you and I,
And will not stand back like cowards
  While the world is moving by."

"*Unitarian, self-reliance,*" said the chaplain, "that same personal responsibility and personal accountability, wholly without reference to what the reliance of all ought to be upon the vicarious sacrifice made by Jesus Christ. It would have exerted a much more healthy influence over your young and developing mind if she had taught you that grand old orthodox hymn, now unfortunately almost obsolete :

"There is a never ending hell,
  And never dying pains,
Where children must with demons dwell,
  In darkness, fire and chains.

Have faith the same with endless shame,
  To all the human race :
For hell is crammed with infants damned
  Without a day of grace."

" Mr. Chaplain, that is positively shocking. The horrors of the battle-field ; the groans of the dying ; the atrocities of the massacre of St. Bartholomew : the Spanish inquisition, and the unparalleled wickedness in the last crusade when Jerusalem was taken, all pale before such a scene. I have never known a man brutal enough to voluntarily supervise an orthodox hell for half an hour, and I am not prepared to believe that God does. Endless misery cannot be reformatory, therefore, the author of endless punishment must be malignant. I have always felt personally responsible for my actions, *believing there was no domain not governed by law*, and that the law, ' Whatsoever a man soweth that shall he also reap ' has no exceptions."

" Who, therefore, was Jesus Christ, and in what way can he do more for humanity

than be a teacher, a beacon light, and
thereby enable us to escape dangerous
rocks and shoals?"

"Why, my dear General, Jesus Christ
was the only begotten son of God, and
he was also the very and eternal God.
His suffering in the garden of Gethsemane and on the cross, 'was in the room
and stead' of all,—"

"Who were elected at that early and
very partisan election?" said the general,
"who accept him?"

"Mr. Chaplain, did Jesus suffer on
those occasions as man, or as God?
Was not Jesus executed in the usual
Roman mode of execution? Was he
recognized after his alleged resurrection by Mary Magdalene, and others?
Was not he supposed to be the gar-
dener? Did he not say in the garden
'If it be possible, let this cup pass from
me, not my will, but thine be done?'
Could he have been addressing himself
when he said thine? Is it not true that

Jesus was born as other children are born, and that his father Joseph was suspicious of illegitimacy; 'for he was minded to put her away privily?' Is it not true that the only evidence of a miraculous conception *was a dream by a man,* his father Joseph? Is it not true that nine other sacred religions have all had similar alleged God origin, and that you reject all of them? Is it not true that Jesus 'grew in stature and increased in knowledge' as other children do? Is it not true that he had the physical weakness, the secretions and excretions of other children? Is it not true that his mother said to him, 'Your *father Joseph* and I have sought you sorrowing?' Is it not true that Jesus disappeared from Palestine at the age of thirteen, and did not reappear for eighteen years? Is it not true that the Golden Rule — the central truth of The Sermon on the Mount, and the highest teaching the world ever knew — was uttered by Confucius in a negative form six hundred and fifty years before Jesus was born, in *a sermon on the mount ?* Is it not true that profane historians assert that it was no uncommon event for men to disappear and reappear after many years? Is it not reasonable that Jesus visited India and obtained the sacred lore of oriental countries? Is it not true that during all the years between the birth of Jesus and his alleged resurrection, that superstition and not reason controlled the people? Is it not true that any phenomenon, however in defiance of reason, was accepted as true if accompanied with signs and wonders; and is it not true that Jesus Christ was a carpenter after his reappearance until a short time before his execution?"

"Yes, General, the Bible is full of mysteries, and of statements that appear to be unreasonable, and I, with my namesake, Calvin, admit the decrees of God

are horrible, but they are in the Bible
and we must accept them."

"Mr. Chaplain, I think the fact that
neither reason, the old or the new testament, if properly translated and understood, nor history, teaches Jesus to have
been God, can be as near demonstrated
as any truth lying outside of pure mathematics. It is a fact the wily and hypocritical Emperor Constantine, who had
been both a Unitarian and Trinitarian as
best suited his purpose at the time, finally
became a Trinitarian, and gave the coloring of Trinitarianism to the teaching
during his reign, which was the immediate cause of the bloody dissensions that
followed, and the remote cause of the
blood-shed that has disgraced Christianity since. Much of the dark and
bloody.record of Christianity, and its intolerance; the massacre of St. Bartholomew, and the Spanish inquisition, which
in Spain alone sacrificed in the most
bloody and brutal manner a thousand a

year for three centuries, of her best men,
should be recognized as the legitimate
fruitage of Trinitarianism, and its intolerant dogmas thrust into the pure teachings of Jesus by Constantine, *and the
low relative position of Spain among
nations to-day is an inexorable sequence.
Jesus as a* MAN commands the honor and
homage of the world. Reason rebels
against the conception of Jesus as God,
he having been born, died, was sometimes disappointed, and asserted that
there were some things he did not know.
The great and eternal God, who fills the
immensity of boundless space with his
presence, and is the soul of every mole-
cule and of every aggregation of mole-
cules; who created our solar system and
all the systems of our nebulae, and the
grand centre around which they all re-
volve, and all the remote nebulae, that have
been, and are being evolved into suns
and planetary systems, *a man*, is to me
the culmination of imbecile and sacrileg-

ious thought. I do not use the word creation in the orthodox sense of the creation of matter out of nothing. The law of conversion of energy. rigidly excludes both creation and annihilation. God created all solar systems in obedience to the law of cosmic evolution outlined by Hume, and elaborated by La Place in the Neubular Hypothesis. And he created man, by the continuous operation through millions of years through the force of organic evolution, from the lowest to the highest organism by the adjustment of internal conditions to the environment, as outlined by the immortal Darwin, *and the absence of links proves the existence of the chain.* The Christian and the natural philosopher of to-day may dwell amid conceptions which beggar those of Milton, in contemplating the works of Deity. Look at the integrated energies of the world —the stored power of our coal-fields, our winds and rivers, our fleets, our armies, and our guns. They are all generated by a portion of the sun's energy that does not amount to a two billion, three hundred millionth of the whole. This is the entire fraction of the sun's force intercepted by the earth, and we convert but a small fraction of this fraction into mechanical energy. Multiplying all our powers by millions of millions we do not reach the sun's expenditure. And yet, notwithstanding this enormous drain, we are unable to detect a diminution of his store. Measured by our highest terrestrial standards such a reservoir of power is infinite, but it is our privilege to rise above these standards, and to regard the sun himself as a speck in infinite extension—a mere drop in the universal sea. We pass to other systems, and other suns, each pouring forth energy like our own, but without infringement of the law, which reveals immutability in the midst of change. · Waves may change to ripple and rip-

ple to waves — magnitude may be sub-
stituted for number, and number for
magnitude — nebulæ may aggregate to
suns, suns may invest their energy in
flora and fauna, and flora and fauna may
melt into air — the sweep of power is
eternally the same.' It rolls in music
through the ages, and the manifestations
of organic life, as well as the display of
physical phenomena are but the modu-
lations of the rythm of the force of nature
controlled and directed by their author,
God, before whom we bow in awe, wonder and admiration. *Reason, therefore,
is appalled at the belief that Jesus was
God.*"

"Well, General," said the chaplain,
"your scholarly attainments and your
enthusiastic defense of your position
delights me. You are, however, more a
lawyer and a soldier than a judge. You
appear to have carried my whole line of
breast-works by your masterly assault,
but you will find that in my position —

the Godship of Jesus — when you consult the Bible, that I am so firmly entrenched that my forces are absolutely invulnerable. The most conclusive evidence of the Lordship of Jesus — that he was a Messiah — is found in the prophecy of the Old Testament, and it amounts almost to a demonstration. It is found in Isaiah, the ninth chapter and the sixth verse, and reads, 'Unto ye a child is born; unto us a son is given. The government shall be upon his shoulders, and his name shall be Wonderful Counselor, the Mighty God, the Everlasting Father, the Prince of Peace.' What stronger evidence could any reasonable man want? There is also the strongest corroborative evidence in the New Testament."

"Mr. Chaplain, my own knowledge of the original language warrants me in saying, there is no reason whatever for believing the prophet had Jesus in his mind when he uttered it. The English

translation of that passage is faulty; it
does not refer to an incarnate Deity, but
simply to a human king. The words
Mighty God and Everlasting Father,
which seem to indicate Deity, should be
left out and other words used in their
places referring to a man. Therefore,
the strongest proof of the Godship of
Jesus in the Old Testament fades away.*

"I know it is believed by many that
Jesus was God, because of the stories
of miraculous birth found in the open-
ing chapters of Mark, Matthew, and
Luke. Legends have grown up around
many of the great men of the past,
especially great religious leaders, as
Budha, Zoroaster, and Moses. Budha
was born of a virgin; so was Fo-hi, the
ancient founder of the Chinese religion.
Zoroaster was miraculously conceived.
Romulus, the founder of Rome, was the

---

* Dr. Briggs, President Harper, Prof. Robert E.
Smith, all believe Isaiah had in his mind the perfect
performance of the ordinary duties of monarchy, and
the new translation also takes that view.

son of the god Mars. Alexander the
Great had a human mother, but his father
was the god Jupiter. The miraculous
birth stories about Jesus are *found only
in Matthew and Luke*; they are not
found in *Mark*, certainly the oldest
Gospel. This fact is suspicious.
Quite as suspicious, too, is the fact
that Jesus himself never refers to any
such miraculous birth. Nobody during
his life-time appears to have known anything about it. If God, and not man,
was his father, and if his birth was
heralded by angels, and attended by miraculous presences, why were his brothers
and relatives so long in believing in
him? Even his mother seemed not to
have known the story, that he had no
human father; for she said when he was
lost in the temple, 'Thy father Joseph
and I have sought thee sorrowing.'
Those miraculous birth stories are the
legendary accretions that gathered about
the history of Jesus long after his

death; after the compilation of the
Gospel of Mark. It would be a marvelous thing if the histories of Abraham
Lincoln left out the fact that he was
president of the United States during
this awful war, and yet, it would not be
a thousandth part so marvelous or so
unaccountable as that the supreme God
of the universe should incarnate himself in Jesus of Nazareth and dwell on
the earth thirty-three years for the purpose of making himself and his salvation known to men, and then should
allow the histories of the time and the
biography of the man in whom he was
incarnated to be so written as to convey
to the future ages no clear idea of who
he was and what he had done. In the
most authentic gospels — Matthew,
Mark, and Luke — Jesus clearly and
repeatedly states that he is *not God.*
Very grave doubts are entertained by
the best scholars whether the Gospel of
John came from his pen, or from any

disciple, and some of the most learned
believe the evidence is irresistible that
it did not. My own investigations lead
me to believe it is not genuine. Jesus'
own declarations found in all the gospels.
that he is not God, ought to be accepted
as final. Among them are found such
passages as: 'My Father is greater than
I. I can of mine own self do nothing;
the words which I speak unto you I
speak not of myself. but of the Father
that dwelleth in me. He doth these
works. My meat is to do the will of
Him that sent me; of that day and
hour knoweth no man, no, not the
angels which are in heaven, neither the
son, but the Father.' 'Why callest
thou me good? there is none good
but one, that is God.' 'I ascend unto
my Father; to my God and your God.'
Jesus always prays to another as God,
and teaches his disciples to pray to
God and not to himself. When a youth
he was spoken of as 'increasing in wis-

dom and stature, and in favor with God
and man.' He was tempted; he mingled
with men as himself a man; he suffers
as others suffer; he weeps as others
weep; he is disappointed as others are
disappointed, as, for example, at the fig
tree. Jesus had his hours of discour-
agement and gloom, as other men have.
On the cross he exclaimed: 'My God,
my God, why hast thou forsaken me?'
The alleged miracles of Jesus have no
weight as evidence in proving him to
have been God. All remarkable persons in those days wrought miracles,
and the Bible represents Elijah as raising the dead. There is no evidence
whatever that the disciples regarded
Jesus as more than a man. At one
time Peter rebuked him; in the garden
of Gethsemane all the disciples forsook
him and fled; during the trial of Jesus,
Peter denied him; on the day of Pen-
tecost, Peter coolly began that remarkable discourse, 'Jesus of Nazareth,

a man approved of God, among you, by
miracles and signs and wonders, which
God did by him.' The alleged miracles
of the resurrection of the body of
Jesus, in the orthodox sense, must be
rejected. The resurrection of a human
body is a scientific impossibility, and, as
the laws of nature have never been
departed from, it has always been an
impossibility. The prophetic view —
the scientific use of the imagination, as
Tyndall would say — of Paul when he
referred to the spiritual body, may have
embodied a great truth lying at present
among the unsolved problems, which,
when solved, may clear up some of the
inconsistencies of orthodoxy. There
are reasons for believing that there
exists an attenuated, ethereal, *material
body,* the exact counterpart of the visible body, and that this spiritual body is
evolved at death, and that it carries on
the complex order of motion that constitutes physical life. There are unmis-

takable evidences of cataclysmic evolution; the most beautiful butterfly is
evolved from the most hideous worm.
It is, therefore, neither unreasonable
nor unscientific to believe that this
spiritual body may be so attenuated
that the laws of inertia may not affect
it. The inertia of matter diminishes as
its density diminishes; thought is without inertia. In imagination I go to the
moon; I step from mountain range to
mountain range; I descend into the
deepest crater, and ride the stream of
lava as it belches forth and flows down
the mountain side. I go to the planet
Saturn, and accompany its moons in
their rapid revolutions; I walk its rings,
I explore its mountains and find the
sources of its rivers. I am at Alcyone,
the grand center of our stellar system,
and contemplate the harmony of the
millions of suns and their planetary
systems. I am at that magnificent constellation, Orion, and explore it in its

6

minutest details; all without the violation of natural law, if the ethereal body
is sufficiently attenuated to be liberated
from the thralldom of inertia.

"While it is true that the gospels, the
epistles and the Acts portray Jesus not as
God, but as a being whom we, in our less
imaginative, less dreamy and more clear
thinking, find some difficulty in always
putting in the category of man, but he
is never represented as God. 'Him
hath God ordained; him hath God sent
forth; him hath God raised up.' Paul
says there is one God, and one mediator
between God and man, the *man* Christ.
Jesus. The old passage in I John,
'There are three that bear witness in
heaven, the Father, the Word and the
Holy Ghost, and these three are one,' is
an interpolation, and ought to be rejected as spurious.*

"Mr. Chaplain, there is probably nothing in the whole Bible that sheds such a

* The revised version omits it.

flood of light on the deity of Jesus, as
the Epistle of James. James was no
doubt the brother of Jesus, brought up
in the same house, *and there is not even
a hint in the epistle that Jesus was God.
A fact of such transcendant importance,
the most important in all the history of
the world, would not have been* left out if
the facts had justified it.

"Herodotus tells us that the Egyptians
believed their god, Osiris, had incarnated
himself in the human form, and dwelt
among men.

"The Chinese believe that Lao-tse existed from all eternity, but descended to
earth, was born of a virgin, lived a human
life and at death ascended to heaven.
Brahmanism is full of the incarnation
idea. Vishnu is believed to have been
incarnated *nine* times. Buddha was an
incarnation of God. In the Greek and
Roman world, too, in the midst of which
Christianity had its birth, and early development, we find essentially the same

thought everywhere. The theological lore of the East had obtained a foothold in Palestine before Jesus' teachings began. The minds of the people were full of the belief in gods in the form of men, and also of men deified, or raised to the condition of gods. All of the Roman emperors, for a period of time, were raised to divine honors. Seutonius informs us that the people fully believed in the divinity of Julius Cæsar. Marcus Aurelius was still worshiped in the time of Diocletian. Antonius was adored in Egypt a century after his death. From Cæsar to Constantine, sixty persons in all were deified. Constantine was doubly deified; he was apotheosized by the pagans, and canonized by the Christians, and coins were stamped having on them a monogram signifying Jesus, Mary and Constantine. The permanent crystallization of these legends and dogmas has ossified the religious spirit of Christianity. Its ethical spirit is that which it has

in common with other sacred religions.
And if its dogmas are properly recognized as symbolical they are beautiful
and true, but if taken in their literal
meaning they commit us to irrational ab-
surdities. Any man who believes the
letter of a myth, or a dogma, or a religious allegory is a pagan, and Christian
paganism is not less absurd than any
other paganism."

" Well, General, I shall not attempt to
reply to you to-day; there is not time, as
the dinner hour is approaching, but shall
we not have a season of prayer before
I go?"

" No, Chaplain, I do not believe it the
time or place for prayers. While I have
permitted a few seasons of prayer here,
I will not do so again. Your prayers
are not as broad as humanity; they appear to me to be needlessly sectional,
and prayers have as little effect in the
recovery of the wounded as they do in
battle, and experience has taught us that

Napoleon was right when he said, 'God was on the side of the best infantry and the heaviest artillery.' In that statement Napoleon showed no disrespect for prayer, any more than did Professor Tyndall's prayer gauge in his Belfast lecture. Neither one of them intended to crush the spirit of devotion that wells up in every human heart, but to show the absurdity of asking for anything in violation of the laws of matter. Do not misunderstand me. I have profound respect for prayer. I often pray, and I am always helped and strengthened by it, but I have never derived any perceptible help from public prayers. I pray as my mother and Jesus did, in secret."

"Of course you pray to our Lord Jesus."

" No, I never pray to Jesus. I would as leave pray to Buddha, from whom Jesus learned much of his teaching. I pray to God to enable me to live like Jesus. I suppose I am selfish in my prayers, for

I rarely take anyone to God but myself, and I never make suggestions to Him."

After the chaplain was gone, a Confederate colonel, who occupied the cot on the other side of the aisle, said: " General, I have been deeply interested in your conversation. I wish to thank you, and I hope such feasts will come often. I have not given the teaching of the Bible careful study as you have, but I have thought a little along that line, and I have been even more surprised at the prayers of the chaplain of my regiment than at yours. How God is able to answer prayers on both the Union and the Confederate side I can't understand, any more than I can comprehend how God is able to give favorable winds at the same time to two vessels at sea going in opposite directions. On the morning of the day on which we were both wounded, my chaplain requested prayers. In his prayer he said : 'This Godless and lawless mob from the north, more vile in

every way than the Goths and Vandals
who swept down upon and destroyed
Rome. must be treated as enemies of God
and man.   They have crossed our sacred
thresholds and are spreading desolation
over our fair land.   They must fall by
the sword. and God will help you bring
upon each and all of them just retribution.   Spare them not. an angry God will
support you in the bloody work of annihilation.'   I did not think much about it
then. but it shocks me to think of it now.
for you appear to me like a younger
brother. and I would not only not shed
a drop of your blood, but I would stand
between you and harm at the peril of my
life."

CHAPTER V.

"Well, Dick," said Wallace, "I have never known you quiet so long at one time before; are you sick or are you thinking of something important?"

"I am well, General, and I have been thinking of your theological discussion. I think the subject a very important one, but very unimportant what I think about it. I have been much more pleased with your scientific and philosophical discussion of the ethics of Christianity than I am with the whiz of minie balls. I am pretty well satisfied with my surroundings, and I am not in a hurry to leave this hospital. Of course, I know my good grub and nice quarters are because I am your orderly, and I am grateful to you for both."

"No, Dick, we cannot remain here much more than a few days longer. My leg is almost well, your commission as major came yesterday and you must be mustered to-morrow. We shall be in the front in a few days. But, Dick, did you hear what was said on the subject of prayer?"

"Yes, General, and I was especially interested while that subject was under consideration. I never thought much about who I prayed to, or what I prayed for: I just prayed, and I always felt better: that was all I knew about it. I suppose I am awfully selfish and narrow in my prayers; although I pray every day, I only remember to have prayed for myself and one other person since I came into the army."

"Well, Dick, I am curious to know who that person was."

"Well, General, as you ask, of course I must tell you, and if I have done wrong I will not do so again. General,

you have been everything to me since I
came to your regiment; I said to you
once before, no one noticed me but you.
Without your kindness to me and my
daily prayers I could not have lived,
and more than that, your high ideas of
right and your fearless and unswerving
adherence to your exalted ethics has
strengthened me day by day, and as I
was not able to return to you anything
for so many kindnesses and favors, I
could only remember you in my prayers,
and I always ask God to bless and protect you."

"Dick, come and sit near me and give
me your hand. Why, it is as soft and
plump as a girl's. I thank you with all
my soul. One of your prayers more
than pays for all I ever did for you.
Your prayers go straight to God and
carry with them a benediction. But,
Dick, have you really been happy during the two months we have been here,
surrounded by the suffering in this hos-

pital ? The groans of the suffering and
the dying, and the pitiful looking for
letters from home and the tearful disap-
pointments, has often moved me to
tears."

"Yes, General, notwithstanding all,
I have been comparatively happy. I
sometimes think it is wicked to feel so,
but it is true. I have been with you all
of the time except when I was writing
letters for some one to their friends and
loved ones at home. I have dressed
your leg every day, and you never
scolded me, *not even once*, and you
almost every time said, 'thank you,
Dick,' so kindly that I almost forgot
my surroundings. I have had a good
room, and, as you know, have had my
meals at the officers' table. My heart
has been almost broken every day, but
I have enjoyed writing letters for the
poor boys. The death of that Confederate major yesterday was deeply
affecting. The captain of the same

regiment, who occupied the next cot to
his, told me that the major was affianced
to a beautiful and accomplished southern lady, whose name was Helen, and
they were to have been married in a few
months, and that she died a few days
before the battle. It was believed that
her death was the cause of his needless
recklessness on the battle-field. He
suffered intensely from the wound in
his spine, and was delirious a large part
of the time. Even when almost writh-
ing in agony, he often urged me to
write to Helen; when I asked for her
address he said, 'She is in heaven;
write to her quickly and I will take the
letter to her.' When the icy fingers of
the grim monster were upon him, in his
delirium he seemed to see her near him,
and he exclaimed, 'O, Helen, I am so
glad you are here!' He extended both
arms, embraced some imaginary object
and pressed his arms firmly to his
breast, a smile of peace and serenity

came over his face and his soul left the
body with Helen in his arms. I know,
General, of the 132 who were in this
ward after the battle, only twenty-three
now remain : they are gone, not to their
regiment for duty, nor to loved ones
longing for their return at home, but to
a home in heaven, and their remains
now lie in that hallowed spot in the rear
of the hospital. I walk among the
newly made mounds every day, and the
saddest thought suggested to my mind
is by that word, 'unknown,' written in
chalk or kale on a board standing at the
head of the mounds. But the thought
comforts me that that word, 'unknown,'
is only of earth, and that it does not
reach to heaven, and that there is to be
in the sweet bye-and-bye a reunion of
loved ones. Such sadness will not be
permitted to exist forever in God's domain, will it, General ? "

" No, I believe you are right, Dick ;
though the mysteries of life and death

bewilder and sometimes appall me. I
cannot think at the end of the great
sweep of God's plans there will be
unhappiness anywhere. All suffering is
for a purpose, and is reformatory when
viewed from the throne of God. It
will not be eternal. All we can do is
to reverently bow in willing submission
to the demands of the unknown. It
requires three hundred and fifty millions
of years for our solar system to complete a revolution around its grand
center in the Pleiades, and it may require a longer time to fully develop a
human soul. But, Dick — no, I must
say Major now — I believe that a right
life in this world ought not to have any
dependence upon our belief in a continuation of life elsewhere. Virtue ought
to be, and is, its own reward. The
origin of man on the earth is shrouded
in thick darkness, and on his final des-
tiny there are but feeble rays of light,
and even if it be true, as some scientists

believe, that the physical organism
through which life is manifested is
returned to the material universe at
death, never again to be recognized,
and if all the forces of the mind and
soul are re-absorbed by the general
store of force, never again to exist as
an entity, it is still a fact that there
exists a deep and abiding sentimental-
ism in the strongest man : the recollec-
tion of mother, sweetheart and wife
produce an ecstasy of feeling and love
for the right, beautiful and good to
which all other influences and forces
are secondary. In my gloomy and
despondent moments, I speculate that
all mental force is derived from and
co-related with the inorganic forces,
and must share the fate of all else in
nature — eternal change without annihilation — which in all its manifestations,
whether in organic or inorganic nature,
even in the highest realm of thought,
obeys the law of equilibrium of matter

and force. The same force that wells
up in a man as consciousness is seen in
the gentle rivulet as it flows onward
toward the ocean, and in the rushing
torrent; in the ocean waves as they
dash against the rock-girt shore; in
the gentle breeze, in the trade winds,
and in the incalculable force of the
cyclone and in the lightning flash.
Even if that be true, man's intellectual
and moral home ought to be far up
among the snow-capped peaks of purity,
honor and culture, so that all will ex-
claim, ' *Ecce Homo!* ' "

"Well, Dick, there comes our commander, the general who brevetted us
on the battle-field."

" Good-morning, General Wallace; I
am glad to find you out of bed; how
are you?"

"Thank you, General, I am almost well.
My wound is healed, and the bone is
quite strong. I yet have a little pain
when I walk, but I will be ready for duty

7

in a few days. General. do you remember my orderly. Dick Dale, whom you brevetted major for gallantry in action? —his commission has arrived and he is a fully developed major now."

"Yes. Major. I remember you well. and I will not soon forget your girlish face. I am glad to see you. as I am always glad to see soldiers of courage and dash in action. You merited your promotion and you will not stop with the rank of major."

The major blushed like a girl in acknowledgment of the compliment.

"But. Wallace." said the General, "I see that hole in your pant leg has not healed. if the hole in your leg has."

"No, General. it has not, and the surgeon would not let me go to the tailor to have my measure for another pair. so that this is the best, and all. I can do at present."

"Don't apologize," said the general. "for that rent in your pant leg ; you have

no cause to feel ashamed of it. I saw
you when it was made; your face was to
the foe and the bullet entered from the
front and at short range. That's a souv-
enir of the battle of Pittsburg Landing.

" Well, General Wallace, you have
been housed up for more than two months
in this hospital, and while I suppose you
have read everything to be found in the
papers you could get hold of, and as I
have not found time to come and see
you, you cannot know the contemplated
movement in the near future, for the obvious reason, that we keep the real ones
out of the papers if possible. The Union
and the Confederate generals observe
the Napoleonic tactics of trying to make
the other fellow believe he is going to
do just what he does not intend to do.
We are sure, however, that the Confederate forces are concentrating at a point
about forty miles beyond our late battle-
field. There is a movement on foot, in
the air, which when perfected, and if

successful, will give it a place in history
as grand strategy: it does not fall
below gigantic in contemplation. The
enemy in our front hold an important
line to the south, between the extreme
east and the west, and they must not be
given sufficient time to perfect their entrenchment, so as to defy our progress
south through the center of the Confederacy. They must be dislodged at an
early date. A matter of almost vital
importance is that the Mississippi River
be opened so that we can communicate
with the Gulf. All of the force not
needed here are to be sent to the west,
and you are to command a divison, and
for the present to remain with the army
moving south through the center of the
Confederate States. As soon as you are
able I want you to come to the front and
get acquainted with your division. You
will be delighted to know that your old
brigade is in, and forms the center of
the division."

"General," said Wallace, "I am ready now. I can start in an hour. What disposition do you wish to make of Major Dale?"

"I leave that matter wholly to you; you know him better than I do. Give him the position best suited to his ability, and what will best subserve the country's needs. My judgment is, however, that he would be invaluable on your staff. There is nothing he will not do that can be accomplished by man."

"Well, Dick," said Wallace a little later, "I have glorious news for you. I have been given the command of a division, and I intend to make it a corps in the next battle, and I have also been authorized to assign you to whatever duty I wish. You will be on my staff, with the rank of major, and I trust after the next engagement it will be colonel. We are needed at the front now. How soon can you be ready to start?"

"I am ready now," said Dale; "after all I like the smell of powder as well as I do the odor of the hospital."

When General Wallace arrived at camp, the division was in line. Every soldier recognized him on sight, and they knew he was to be their commander. His old brigade was in the center. As he approached and rode the length of the line with the corps commander, who introduced him as "General Wallace, your commander," the wildest enthusiasm prevailed, and the reception given him was as cordial and enthusiastic as would have been given to Napoleon by his Old Guard, after an absence of three months. From all along the line came cheer after cheer, and shouts of "Long live General Wallace!" One enthusiastic soldier from Iowa, with more zeal than elegance in language, whose voice rose above the tumult, shouted: "We can storm hell and Gibraltar before breakfast with General Wallace as our leader!"

The general rode back to the center of the line, removed his hat, and said: "Comrades, I thank you for this manifestation of friendship and confidence. It shall be my constant endeavor to live worthy of a continuation of it."

In a few days marching orders were received, and on the evening of the third day they were in line of battle, with a strong picket line thrown out in front of a strong Confederate force, commanded by an able and intrepid Confederate general.

General Wallace, at a late hour in the night, walked the entire length of the picket line. All of the pickets were walking their lonely beats, except one, who was asleep, and his gun lying by his side. The general took his gun and walked his beat until he waked. He recognized the general at once and was badly frightened. "General," said he, "I know I will be court-martialed and shot and I deserve it, for I know the danger we are in. I am not afraid to die

on the battle-field, but to be shot for neg-
lect of duty will bring awful sorrow to my
poor old father, and disgrace upon me."

The general handed him his gun and
said, "Don't worry. Of course you did
a great wrong; not only your own life,
but the whole army was in danger of a
surprise on account of this post being
vacant, but you had made a long, hard
march, and you were very tired. I will
excuse you this time and will not report
you. You will not do so again."

At daylight the whole line was advanced, and before 8 o'clock the battle
was on. General Wallace's division held
the center of the line, and his old brigade
the center of the division. He rode from
one end of the division to the other every
few minutes, and his horse was never
twenty feet in the rear of the line, dur-
during the entire battle. At one time,
during the fiercest part of the engagement, three Confederate batteries were
hurried into position directly in his front,

supported by three lines of infantry, for
the obvious purpose of breaking the
center of the Union line. Wallace
strengthened the line in the center, and
they moved forward with the steadiness
of veterans, and never wavered or fal-
tered. After four hours' hard and continuous fighting, which was little less
than one continuous charge, the Confederate forces were routed and fled in
every direction and the victory was won,
but the dead and dying attested the
valor of the Confederate soldiers.

Major Dale had not appeared so happy
since he entered the service, as on that
day. He rode from the general to any
and every part of the line in an instant.
His face wore a smile, even when the
three batteries were belching forth grape
and cannister on the center of the line,
and in a hail-storm of minie balls, his
smiling face was everywhere to be seen.
He was nicknamed the "Smiling Major,"
and was ever after known by that name.

CHAPTER VI.

UNWRITTEN HISTORY.

During the next year and a half, up to the beginning of the most remarkable campaign in the history of wars, ancient or modern, with the possible exception of Napoleon's retreat from Moscow, if that disastrous retreat can be called a campaign, the same scenes were enacted on four other bloody battle-fields. At no time in the military life of Wallace, as major, as colonel or as general, did the men under him fail to accomplish all he, as their commander, asked them to do, except in one instance. He was always with his men; his headquarters were in the saddle in every engagement, within speaking distance of the line of battle. He was a firm believer that soldiers would always do their duty if their commander did his, and it is known that

during his military life he never showed
the slightest temper, except when he saw
a brigade, division, or corps commander
establish his headquarters far behind the
line of battle in a place of little danger.
Before the commencement of the memorable campaign before referred to,
which begun on the fourth day of May,
1864, he had been twice brevetted general and Major Dale had been brevetted
colonel.

There are soldiers now living in Iowa
who know the facts, and future and impartial history will develop them. It is
a historic fact that early in the Atlanta
campaign General Sherman directed
McPherson to pass through Snake Creek
Gap and strike the railroad in the rear
of Resaca, which was then strongly for-
tified by Confederate forces, commanded
by the able and intrepid General Johnson, whose force was at that time, and
continued to be during the entire campaign, nearly one-third less than Sher-

man's. It is also a historical fact that
though McPherson was Sherman's favorite general, he was at least mildly criti-
cised by Sherman and others in the army
for not doing that which appeared possible and very desirable. The inevitable
consequences of that movement, which
would have gone into history as grand
strategy if it had been successful, would
have been to have seriously crippled
Johnson, if not have ended the campaign at once. The roads from Resaca
to Atlanta were almost impassable from
heavy rains, and if transportation over
the railroad had been cut off disaster to
Johnson and his army was at hand. The
author was in the army and passed
through Snake Creek Gap among the
first of the forces and he believed then,
and long reflections since, and a careful
analysis of all ascertainable facts,—the
relative size of the Union and Confederate armies and the fact that Johnson did
not anticipate such a movement by Sher-

man, there being almost no Confederate
force at that point,—confirms him in the
belief that Sherman did not ask an unreasonable thing from McPherson. Of
course if something had been done that
was not done, the results of that something cannot be known definitely, but
the logic of events points to the proba-
bility of the attack having been successful.

The unwritten history is, that on
the morning of the first day of the battle of Resaca, while there was heavy
skirmish firing in front of Resaca, about
two or three miles to the left of the
point of which I am speaking, General
McPherson, General Wallace and a part
of their staff rode to an elevated point
from which could be seen with their
glasses the tressel bridge on the railroad
three miles south of Resaca, and while
they were looking a heavy freight train
passed over the bridge going to Resaca.
General McPherson saw the importance

of the destruction of that bridge, but he was undecided as to what to do. If the attack was made and Johnson should evacuate Resaca and throw his whole army on the Union forces about the bridge it would be crushed, and all killed or captured.

General McPherson was one of the best generals in the army, and his usual custom was to ride out to the front, view the surroundings with his glass, and at once determine upon his plans and promptly give his orders. Never before, nor after, up to the memorable 22d of July, was he known to hesitate.

Wallace being a subordinate general, though highly esteemed and appreciated by McPherson, sat quietly on his horse waiting for orders. After a silence that appeared painful to both, Wallace said: "I can burn that bridge in half an hour, and if I and my whole division die in doing it, it will save the lives of many more than there are in my command."

General McPherson, after a few moments, said: "I believe you can burn
the bridge, the small force now guarding
it would be no obstacle for your division, but we can't spare you and your division. The question is, have we the
right to do that which would certainly
imperil all your lives *in the hope* of ac-
complishing even so important an object.
Your division is invincible with any ordinary force in their front, but you
could not withstand the shock of Johnson's whole army. I cannot sacrifice
you. I see your anxiety; there are tears
in your eyes, and I regret I can't give
the order."

What the result would have been can
only be speculated upon, beyond the
fact *that the bridge would have been
burned if the order had been given.* In
speculating upon the immediate and the
remote results if the bridge had been
burned, several circumstances must be
taken into consideration. General Wal-

lace's command up to that time had
never failed to accomplish all of whatever they had undertaken. They had
unbounded confidence in his sagacity
and generalship, as well as in his courage. Johnson's force was inferior to
Sherman's and was then engaged with
Sherman at Resaca; that Johnson would
have evacuated Resaca and hurled his
whole force upon Wallace to protect his
rear, there is scarcely the shadow of a
doubt. McPherson's three corps were
within easy reach, and at the first gun
would have been thrown with destructive
force on the Confederate flank, and when
the roar of the musketry and cannonading
was heard at the bridge, Sherman would
have hurried the Union army through
Resaca and attacked Johnson in the
rear. Even if Johnson had crushed
Wallace and killed or captured his entire command *the bridge would have been
gone,* and it would have been absolutely
impossible for Johnson to have taken

his wagon train and his heavy ordnance over any other road than the one leading south along the railroad. The inevitable result would have been to seriously cripple Johnson, with the probable result of capturing a large part of the Confederate force under him. It is highly probable that even a complete success of the Union force at the bridge would not have ended the campaign at that point, but it would not have been, as it was, a battle that lasted one hundred and twenty days, and a battle-field one hundred and thirty miles long. That desperate, improper and disastrous charge on the Confederate works about Kenesaw, in which Sherman admits he lost a thousand a minute for ten consecutive minutes in killed, would never have been made. The criticism of that charge is not made without foundation, for what was done after could have been done before. Kenesaw was evacuated when it became apparent to Johnson that the railroad in his rear was in danger. The same thing was done at Atlanta, when Sherman's movement on Jonesboro was discovered.

The battle of July 22d before Atlanta was neither desired nor expected by Sherman, but was due to Hood's want of generalship.

It was on that day that General Sherman said : "Johnson is a sensible general, and I can generally know what he is going to do, but Hood, being a damned fool, I never know what he is going to do."

I had a rare opportunity on the 22d to observe the great Sherman during the whole of the battle, rendered especially memorable by the death of McPherson. His headquarters were at the Howard house all day, and my duty also kept me at or near the general from early morning until the close of the battle. I was at leisure most of the time, and there was not ten minutes at any one time that I did not see him. Early in the morning, between seven and eight o'clock, General McPherson rode up to the Howard house. Very soon John A. Logan, General Wallace, General Dodge and General Blair came. Nothing of importance appeared likely to happen. Picket firing in our front and to our right continued as usual, to which no attention was paid; for we all knew our works were invulnerable to the Confederate force in Atlanta. About half past nine Generals Sherman, Wallace, McPherson and Logan were sitting on the porch and Generals Blair and Dodge were standing in front of them; they were joking and laughing; I was near enough to hear every word spoken. At this time quite a heavy musketry was heard to our left, at a point where there was not known to be any Confederate force. The generals appeared to be surprised. General Sherman said : "What does that mean?"

General McPherson said:

"I will find out."

He mounted his horse and rode into the woods in the direction of the firing. He was followed by Logan, Dodge, Blair and Wallace, and in half an hour the great battle of Atlanta was on.

The battle raged, with occasional lulls, all day. The thunder of the artillery and the roll of the musketry came nearer and then receded, again and again, so that the awful problem as to who was to be victorious was not solved until late in the evening. That day appeared to me the longest day of my life; I thought of Wellington, "Oh, for Blucher or night!" and of the sun standing still for Joshua. The sun appeared to be standing in the heavens. Late in the afternoon our lines were temporarily driven back, and the outlook was that the Howard house and the temporary hospital would fall into the hands of the Confederates. We were so near the line of battle that many stray bullets struck the house and fell among the wounded.

General Sherman's great soul was tempest-tossed all day after the battle begun. He was nervous and uneasy; he walked the porch and looked toward the battle-field with an expression of awful anxiety, but no word came until the body of McPherson was brought in on a stretcher. The final charge was made by Wallace's division, and it was like the mad rush of the tempest, as irresistible as the cyclone.

The battle of the 28th was disastrous to the Confederate army for the same reason that the charge on Kenesaw mountain was disastrous to the Union army—they charged ample fortifications. The 36th Alabama regiment lost every field and line officer, and more than two hundred in that charge. Sherman's subsequent evacuation of all the works about Atlanta; his movement back to the Chattanooga river; his flank movement and the capture of Jonesboro, ended the Atlanta campaign.

The Atlanta campaign will be regarded as a marvel in modern warfare by the impartial historians of the future. All the later movements are worthy the name of grand strategy: he succeeded in wholly misleading the Confederate generals as to what he was going to do.

After the close of the campaign the entire Union army had a few weeks of much needed rest. Wallace's command had suffered severely at Resaca, and he had lost a fourth of his division in the charge on Kenesaw, and his loss was heavy in the battle of the 22d, which necessitated rest and reorganization.

CHAPTER VII

HELL.

A few days after the regiment had gone into camp the chaplain returned to his post of duty. His time for the last four months had been spent in the hospitals caring for the wounded. He had not been with his regiment since the battle of Resaca. He preached a sermon on the first Sunday after his arrival. He sent a note to General Wallace, in which he said: "In view of your success in the campaign just closed, and of your merited promotion, I shall feel myself complimented by your presence."

The general acknowledged the receipt of the letter, thanked him for it, and said: "I feel under deep and lasting obligations to you for the care you have taken of those who were dear to me. I have heard of your devotion to duty, of your sleepless nights, of your care to the poor boys, in dressing their wounds, writing letters for them, and your fatherly kindness in talking with them of home and loved ones. It will give me pleasure to be present at service next Sunday."

He preached from the text, "As in Adam all died, so in Christ are all made alive."

The creation of Adam was miraculous and instantaneous, and a rib was taken from his side while he slept, from which Eve was created. The Garden of Eden was a literal garden, and a fruit orchard attached. In no sense was it allegorical. Sin entered the world, and the condemnation of all was because Adam disobeyed the command of God, and ate of the forbidden fruit. The consequences of that act extended to the most remote ages : all were alike doomed to perdition, and the youngest child had no hope of escape, unless its original sin

was washed away in the blood of Christ.
Without conversion, which was a miraculous change of nature, wrought by God
himself, and the creature was nothing
more than a recipient of the divine favor,
not on account of anything he had done
or could do, but on account of a prede-
termination on the part of Deity, a literal and eternal hell awaited all. He
gave extensive quotations from the sermon by Jonathan Edwards on "The
sinner in the hands of an angry God,"
because the final doom of the impenitent was described in stronger language
than he could command. God's eternal
truths were the same to-day as when
Edwards preached; the same Bible
taught the same awful fate of the unre-
ligious. "They deserve to be cast
into hell: So that divine justice never
stands in the way: it makes no objec-
tion to God's using his power at any
moment to destroy them. They are
already under sentence of condemna-

tion to hell. They are now the object
of that very same anger and wrath of
God that is expressed in the torment of
hell. God is a great deal more angry
with great numbers now on earth, yea
with many now in this congregation,
than he is with those who are now in
the flames of hell. The devil stands
ready to fall upon and seize them as his
own at any moment God shall permit
him. The God that holds you over the
pit of hell, much as one holds a spider
or some loathesome insect over the fire,
abhors you and is dreadfully provoked ;
His wrath toward you burns like fire ;
He looks upon you as worthy of nothing
else but to be cast into hell fire. That
God will execute the fierceness of His
anger, implies that he will inflict wrath
without pity. God will have no other
use to put you to but only to suffer misery. It is the everlasting wrath. It
would be dreadful to suffer this fierceness and wrath of Almighty God one

moment, but you must suffer it to all
eternity. Millions of millions of years
you will writhe in the sulphurous flames
of hell, because of the merciless vengeance of an angry God. But this is
the dismal call of every soul in the congregation that has not been born again,
however moral and strict, sober and
religious they may otherwise have been."

At the close of the sermon, which had
been listened to with stolid indifference
and disgust, he asked a brother chaplain
of another regiment, in the same brigade,
who was an enthusiastic Methodist, to
make a few remarks. He began by saying: "The fiery indignation and wrath
of an insulted and angry God has been
as forcibly portrayed by the brother
as language could do it, but words
utterly fail to represent the fierceness of the flaming fury of an angry
God. The most appalling picture by
the most vivid imagination can at most
be only as a shadow to the substance.

The duration of hell has not been dwelt upon as its importance demands. Even a million of years cannot be grasped by the human mind, but when I say to you that if a bird were to take a leaf from the forest and carry it to Europe, and return and take another, and continue until every leaf in all the forests on the western continent had been removed and that each trip required one hundred years to complete it, and that after that it should take a grain of sand and carry it to Australia, and return and get another, and so on until the western hemisphere had been removed, that at the expiration of that inconceivable period of time *hell had only begun,*— you would have only a feeble representation of the duration of the misery of the damned! The intensity of the heat that envelopes the damned may be feebly represented by the illustration often used by the early fathers in the church. If a soul would be taken from the flames of hell

and transferred to a cauldron of red-hot
potash, the change would be so great
that he would freeze in a few moments.
But all the danger to which you are
exposed and all the consequences of a
wicked life, however vile and depraved
you may have been, and are, can be and
will be removed in an instant if you re-
pent and ask God to forgive you. A
pure, honorable life is no aid in securing
forgiveness: on the contrary it is a barrier."

On the afternoon of the day on which
the sermon was preached Generals Logan, Blair and Dodge called on General
Wallace at his headquarters.

They were very cordially received by
Wallace and Colonel Dale.

"Gentlemen," said Wallace, "I am
especially glad to see you at this time.
Colonel Dale and I were talking of the
many noble qualities possessed by General McPherson, and his tragic death, and
we both became almost melancholy."

Logan said: "The subject under consideration was a grand one, but there are some unfortunate circumstances in connection with his death, well calculated to make his friends despondent. I came very near riding into the same gap. As you remember, we left Sherman's headquarters at the same time. I rode with him until we were near the line of battle, as we supposed; for the bullets were falling around us, but our own troops were not to be seen. I was surprised not to come upon our own soldiers, and I think McPherson also was surprised. He said to me, 'Ride to the left and I will go on to the front.' I did as directed and came in the rear of my corps. He, as we know, rode forward into the gap between the corps, and the first troops seen was the Confederate skirmish line. He was halted, but he wheeled his horse, plunged spurs into his side, expecting to ride out of danger. It is highly probable that his first conception of his situation was when he was halted by the Confederate skirmish line, as there were no Union soldiers in sight, to the right nor to the left. Oh, he was a grand man! One of nature's noblemen! He could not do a mean thing, nor anything that was unkind to any one. He had a heart as big as humanity, and as fearless as a lion, and yet as easily touched in tenderness as a woman's. He was the only regular army officer who did not at some time at least hint to me that he possessed some military qualifications not to be found in any civilian general."

"Yes," said General Dodge, "nature was prodigal to him in bestowing her choicest gifts that constitute the highest type of the American citizen and soldier, and I have found myself many times since his death saying, 'If he had rode twenty rods to the right he would have been in the rear of *my* corps. Even if he made no profession of religion, he

came as near being governed at all times
by the great central truth of the Sermon
on the Mount as any man I ever knew."

" I never saw him exhibit the slightest
temper, except on one occasion," said
General Blair. " We were walking
leisurely through the camp, and, as we
passed the guard-house, a fine, manly
looking soldier was being rather roughly
forced quite against his will into it.
General McPherson said, 'Is that man
a good soldier? what has he done?'
'Yes, general, he is a good soldier, but
he has been foraging without orders;
he brought into camp last night seven
chickens.' 'Open that door!' thundered
McPherson in a rage, 'and send that
man back to his company. I wish it had
been seventy thousand instead of seven.
I would like to see every soldier in the
army have fried chicken for breakfast,
with biscuits and butter.'"

" You all know," said General Wallace, " that McPherson and I were

especial friends. I have been much in his company, and he treated me as a younger brother. His unselfish, and I think I may say Christian, character and life appeared to me inexplicable in a man who was absolutely without fear : his standard of ethics was not below the highest ever taught by man, and their exemplification was his daily life. I shall never forget our last social meeting ; it was three or four nights before the 22nd, and we remained together until after 1 o'clock. He was in every sense a scholarly general ; his familiarity with ancient generals and campaigns equaled that of a professor in ancient history. I seem now to hear his philosophical discussion on the great campaigns of Alexander the Great, and to see his noble face as he speaks of that rapid march to Thebes, and to listen to his justification of the execution of 30,000, and to the sale of 30,000 more into perpetual slavery. Demos-

9

thenes was then in Athens, and he was
a deadly enemy of the young king.
Less severity would not have prevented
revolt during his contemplated absence:
he left Greece soon thereafter and never
returned: he died in Babylon ten years
later, and peace was continous in Greece
until after his death. His social defects
were not the faults of the man, but of
the times in which he lived. The strategy of Hannibal, his fate and his brilliant generalship were ever fresh in his
mind, and the campaigns of Cæsar and
Pompey were vividly portrayed. Napoleon was his ideal of a military hero:
his gigantic plans, his surpassing strategy and the faultless execution of his
campaigns were marvels in the art of
war. He said in our last conversation:
'I am as firm a believer in the preservation of our identity after death as was
Napoleon. The soul is not changed,
but takes with it its disposition, habits
and tendencies. I shall, upon my en-

trance into the spiritual life, whenever
that may be, first seek the company of
the greatest military minds of the world,
ancient and modern,' and then Jesus,
whom I believe to have been the greatest and most wonderful man the world
ever produced. As I have been so delighted with your scholarly research
about his life up to the time he began
to teach in Galilee, the reasonableness
of his association with teachers in the
far East gives to his life and teaching
additional interest."

" Come in, Mr. Chaplain," said General
Wallace, as that gentleman appeared at
the door. "This gentleman is my esteemed friend, Mr. Calvin, the chaplain of
my regiment — General Logan, General
Blair and General Dodge; you need no
introduction to Colonel Dale. We have
been talking of General McPherson, and
I have not been able to rid myself of
the feeling that you had him in your
mind during your sermon yesterday."

"I did not," said the chaplain, "have the honor of a personal acquaintance with the general. I am informed, however, that he was one of the noblest of men; that he was all any unconverted man could be; but, gentlemen, God will not change His plans of salvation even for General McPherson. I understand that he was not only *an unconverted man,* but that he did not even believe conversion was necessary to salvation; that he trusted in a right life. He therefore gave no evidence that he was one of the elect. It is not I who shall judge him, but God. Sad as is the thought to me, and even more sad to you, his personal friends and admirers, there is no hope for him. There is but one way of salvation, and that he rejected. He is beyond doubt at this moment bewailing his awful fate."

"General McPherson in hell!" said Wallace, the fire of indignation flaming from his eyes. "Outrageous! infam-

ous! damnable! He lived a Christian
life unconsciously; he was an heir of
heaven by birthright, and he never for-
feited that right by a wicked life. True,
he never made any *profession of religion*,
nor was it necessary; *he lived it.* He
was one of the ninety and nine who had
never gone astray. Such a man in hell!
The thought is enough to make angels
weep and the damned rejoice. That
greatest truth ever uttered by man, viz.:
'Whatsoever ye would that man should
do unto you, do ye even so to him," was
the inspiration of his life, and would
have been evolved by him if it had not
been given to the world before. Was
that loving apostle, James, the brother
of Jesus, ignorant of what constituted
religion? Is it a fact that pure, unde-
filed religion before God is to visit the
widows and the orphans in their affliction, and to keep one's self unspotted
before the world? Or is it a snare and
a delusion given to the world by Jesus

and his apostles? Are we to have any
respect for the statement made by Jesus
Christ when he said. ' By this ye shall
know that you are my disciples, *if you
love one another?* ' Does the broad statement. large as humanity. that, 'in every
nation he that feareth God and worketh
righteousness *is* accepted of him.' mean
nothing? "

  " General." said the chaplain, " it required great courage to preach that
sermon, and at this time. in the presence
of the generals of this army, holding as
you do. the welfare of the nation in
your hands. requires more courage than
I of myself possess. but aided as I have
been. and am. from above. I am able to
say, I cannot retract a word of that sermon. On the contrary, it is my duty as
a minister of the gospel to emphasize
the statements then made. Depend
upon it. gentlemen, the Bible is a holy
and infallible book, written every word
and line by the hand of God; it must

be accepted as it reads, literally ; not
with the alleged rationalistic interpretation given by some modern scholars, whose rendering in some instances
encourages a skepticism more dangerous
than the avowed infidelity of Thomas
Paine and Voltaire. I refer particularly
to the scholarly, but pernicious, teaching of Theodore Parker, and the brilliant
star, James Freeman Clark. The Bible
justifies the fiery denunciation made by
Jonathan Edwards of the impenitent —
the non-elect — and the same personal
devil is impassionately waiting to claim
his own."

"Mr. Chaplain," said Wallace, "the
belief in the infallibility of the Bible
has been one of the leading causes in
producing the spirit of intolerance
manifested by all orthodox churches.
It has made the history of Christianity
a history of bloodshed ; it was the cause
of the brutal assassination of the loving
Servitis by the cold-blooded and intol-

lerant Calvin, and of the fierce conflicts
between science and religion in the
domain of philosophy, and geology,
which resulted in the slow and inhuman
punishment of Galileo, rendered doubly
so because of his age and infirmities,
and of the infamous burning of Bruno.

"No sentence ever uttered by man
has caused so much misery and death as
that found in the Bible, viz., 'Suffer not
a witch to live.' Neither Nero, Robes-
pierre nor Bloody Mary ever uttered
language that equaled it in producing
wholesale murder.

"Mr. Chaplain, I admit the truth of
your oft-repeated statement that the
'Catholic Church has been intolerant.'
And it is also true that this intolerant
spirit has been transmitted to her Protestant offspring in a most aggravated
form.

"Protestantism has been the deadly
foe of mental liberty, and of progress in
many instances. Beneath the cloak of

friendship Christianity has carried the assassin's dagger and the fagot, for any bold thinker who attempted to burst the bars of an imprisoning creed. Bigotry tortured and the church murdered.

" Scarcely had the Reformation gained a foothold in Germany before Protestants began their work of bloody persecution against Catholics ; and when they became stronger and divided into sects, against each other. It was Protestants who at the point of the sword made the people of Saxony and Bradenburg renounce the Catholic faith ; it was Protestants who drove the inhabitants of Munster from their homes in the dead of winter. The fanatical Munzer overran Germany, preaching and plundering, baptizing and butchering until forty thousand perished in his mad attempt to make Anabaptists of Lutherans and Catholics. The tables were turned. Munzer was captured and put to a bloody death, and his 'Religious Revival'

was succeeded by a protracted effort on
the part of Lutherans. 'As long as
there is a drop of blood in your veins,'
pursue as wild beasts and consume like
wolves these miserable peasants,' was
the command of Martin Luther. For
months the bloody work of an effort at
annihilation continued at Wernsburg,
Alsatia, Bande, and thousands of peasants fell victims to their relentless fury.

"The violent dissensions between
Luther and Zwingle, and subsequently
between Luther's disciples and Calvin,
and the bloodshed which those dissensions produced is known to every student of history.

"In the Netherlands the Calvinists
destroyed the Catholic churches, butch-
ered the priests, and even dragged the
bodies of the dead from their graves.
'For three nights and two days,' says
the history, 'did the havoc rage un-
checked through the city of Antwerp
and all the neighboring villages. Scarcely

a work of art escaped destruction. On
every hand were the ruins of churches,
broken statues, torn pictures, and murdered priests.'

"In Holland, the Protestant leader,
Sonoy, imprisoned, tortured and slaugh-
tered thousands for no other crime than
that of being Catholics.

"Motley, in his 'Rise of the Dutch
Republic,' cites the following among
many other instances of Sonoy's cruelty:

"'Nanning Koppezoon was a man in
the full vigor of his years. He bore
with perfect fortitude a series of incred-
ible tortures, after which, with his body
singed from head to heel, and his feet
almost entirely flayed, he was left for
six weeks to crawl about his dungeon
on his knees. He was then brought
back to the torture-room and again
stretched upon the rack, while a large
earthen vessel, made for the purpose,
was placed inverted upon his naked
body. A number of rats were intro-

duced under the cover and hot coals were heaped upon the vessel until the rats, rendered furious by the heat, gnawed into the very bowels of the victim in their agony, to escape. The holes thus torn in his bleeding flesh were filled with red-hot coals. He was afterward subjected to other tortures too foul to relate; nor was it until he had endured all this agony with a fortitude which seemed supernatural that he was at last discovered to be human. Scorched, bitten, dislocated in every joint, sleepless, starving, perishing with thirst, he was at last crushed into a false confession by a promise of absolute forgiveness.'

"But if Koppezoon believed that a spark of honor existed in the breast of this Protestant persecutor, he was soon convinced of his error. He was permitted to live long enough to see his aged father die upon the rack, when his own heart was torn from his bosom and

thrust into his face, his head was taken
off and placed on the church steeple of
his native village and his body quar-
tered and exposed upon the towers of
Alkamaar!

"The Protestant Church of England
was probably the most intolerant of all
churches. Its footsteps are marked
with blood; its victims were put to
the most frightful tortures before
they were executed — tortures that for
their fiendish refinement would have
brought a smile of satisfaction to the
face of Torquemada.

"The following is one example of
daily scenes that were enacted while
Protestant power was supreme in England during many years:

"A Mrs. Clithero perishes at York.
She is a lady of high character, and her
sole offense is having afforded refuge to
a famishing priest. The mode of death
is as follows: She is placed on the
floor on her back, with her hands and

feet firmly bound. A heavy door is laid upon her, and enormous weights placed upon the door. Sharp stones have been put under her body, and the weights pressing down force these through the flesh, breaking her ribs, causing hours of intense agony and finally death. It seems scarcely possible for heartless cruelty to be carried farther; and yet these Protestants, not content with inhumanly murdering this poor mother, brutally beat her weeping children that stand around her bruised and mangled corpse, and throw the eldest, only twelve years old, into prison."

"Yes, General," said the chaplain, "the history of Christianity is a history of barbarity and bloodshed from which angels would turn away with tears in their eyes, *but that black record is the history of the acts of men,* prompted to, and sometimes goaded on, by former persecutions not in any instance in keeping with the teaching of Jesus Christ."

"Mr. Chaplain, there is no difference between us upon that point. The pure and loving teaching of Jesus never caused a tear, and will redeem the world, if accepted, *but the fact remains that the atrocities of history were done in the name of Christianity, because the perpetrators of those crimes believed* THEIR *interpretations of the Bible to be infallible.*

"The belief in the existence of a personal devil, — whose machinations and plans have thwarted God in the care of the ninety per cent of the human family, who goes around roaring like a lion seeking whom he may devour,— is still dear to the clergy who have been side-tracked while the train of progress passed them. No fact of science is better established, or more universally accepted by the scholars of the world, than that there is in the entire universe of God *but one original force, God.* The law of the conserva-

tion of energy is a demonstration of the
eternal truth that the controlling and
directing power is in *one* personality, or
in one entity above personality, and not
in two. 'Getting religion.' Mr. Chaplain, is nothing but emotional slush,
often depending upon a morbid stomach
and liver, in other cases a morbid brain,
poisoned in early years by false and
pernicious teaching. The great doctrine of the Atonement, as you dignify
it, is referred to but once in the whole
Bible, and the proper rendering of the
word used in that place means, *at one*
with Jesus Christ, nothing more; and
the same principle of a right life per-
vades the entire New Testament. No
honorable man ought to desire or expect
anything beyond what he merits, and it
would require as high manhood as I
have ever seen to prevent, at least, indifference about our conduct if some
other person, whom we had never seen,
was to suffer the consequences of our

sins. Where, therefore, is there any
authority for the emotional gush called
a change of heart, or conversion, which
is generally exhibited by those of a
cowardly nature, conscious of having
lived a wicked life? And where was
there ever a shadow of a foundation for
that infamous doctrine of 'election,'
when the Bible specifically states, 'God
is no respecter of persons?' The beneficence and the eternal justice of the
inviolable law of heredity embodied in
that wonderful passage — wonderful because of the time it was given to the
world in the Bible — viz., 'Be not deceived: God is not mocked; whatsoever a man soweth, that shall he also
reap,' is confirmed by the observation
and experience of every thinker. Esau
sold his birthright for a mess of pottage,
and though he sought it diligently with
tears, he never found it again. Every
account run with retribution must be
settled in this world, or in some other

world.   God never encouraged a wicked life with the assurance that an innocent person would suffer the legitimate consequences thereof.   The whole threadworn theory of conversion or a change of heart, embracing the fall of man and salvation through the blood of Christ, is an irrational dogma, thrust into the pure teaching of the great Master, more than 300 years after his death, by the Council of Nice.   *There never was a fall.*   Anthropology has demonstrated that man has arisen everywhere from low and brutal conditions, and the unmistakable teaching of the Bible, approved by common sense, is that salvation is obtained in no other way than by a right life. The God of heaven and earth never intended that any person should find license for sinning in the belief that future repentance will wipe out the willful transgressions of the past.   The law that a man shall reap what he sows is a law of infinite blessing, because it

fosters good and warns against evil. It
encourages the formation of character.
There should be no difference of opinion that the life-work of Jesus was to
redeem man from his sins, and not to re-
move the consequences of sins. Mr.
Calvin, the religion of the future will
recognize the fact that man is on the
earth for discipline, and that all pain
and suffering, in this or any other world,
has a preservative function. The beneficence of the pain produced when a
child, unconscious of the fact that fire
burns, puts its dimpled hand against the
hot stove is easily understood to be a
lesson in an education, and to be preservative in its influence. The secret
of pain is progress. Look where you
please, and you will find gleaming
through the shadow of suffering the
light of a gracious purpose of progress
through pain. Science unites with
philosophy and religion in revealing
this goal of our costly progress. Mr.

Darwin declares, in his 'Origin of Species,' as natural selection works solely by and for the good of each individual, that the physical and mental endowments will tend to progress toward perfection. It follows that all evil must gradually disappear from human life, as imperfection grows out toward perfection. Mr. Herbert Spencer looks forward to the diminution of human ills, and to their entire disappearance in the far future. The vision of science and philosophy is of a coming man, redeemed by pain from pain, educated through suffering out of suffering, not because of any arbitrary decree, but by and through the continuous operation of the law of evolution. All of the suffering, therefore, of individuals and of aggregations of individuals is simply the penalty for violated law, *and is always reformatory,* and as the entire domain of God is governed by law, not in conflict with

what we recognize around us, the same
is true in all worlds, now and in the
future. Our inability to see more than
a short segment of the circle in the
great sweep of infinite goodness demands of us a modest faith, based upon
reason, or, as Professor Tyndall would
say, 'the scientific use of the imagination.'"

A loud rap is heard at the door. A
colonel from General Sherman's staff
enters with the following order:

HEADQUARTERS: *Generals Howard, Blair, Logan,
Wallace, Dodge* — General Hood and the Confederate
army are moving to the north. Come at once.

SHERMAN.

CHAPTER VIII.

THE following conversation between General McPherson and General Wallace occurred early in July. 1864, near Atlanta, Georgia:

General McPherson said: "You know from my frequent calls, often without business, that I am delighted with your company. As a conversationalist you possess rare gifts. Your charming talks of your travels in the East are to me especially interesting. With your permission, I will ask Generals Sherman, Logan, Dodge. Blair. Howard and a few of my favorite colonels to my headquarters some evening to hear a lecture from you upon that subject. Personally I would be delighted with a repetition of your reasons for believing Jesus to have spent the time he was absent from his native land in oriental countries."

"General McPherson," said Wallace, "I appreciate the high compliment, and as it is your request, it shall be granted. You may designate the evening."

THE LECTURE.

" *Mr. President and Gentlemen,*— The honor of addressing a select audience composed of the generals and colonels commanding the Union army, in the midst of one of the remarkable campaigns in the history of wars, with Gen. W. T. Sherman in the chair, is an honor I never dreamed of, much less ever expected to realize. In presenting myself before you, I deeply regret that I am not better prepared to talk to you on the subject indicated. Had I access to the many notes taken during my studies in the East, and the many valuable works of reference by eminent scholars that are now lying packed in my trunk at home, I might have been enabled to make my talk more interesting in point of data and scholarly research.

"Knowing General McPherson's invitation to talk to you this evening to be the result of several conversations with him on religious subjects, I will not burden you with a description of the majestic scenery, the strange people, their queer manners and customs, and the many thrilling and pleasant experiences I met with on my travel through the countries of the Orient, but will endeavor to confine myself to the religions of its people, and give you some of the points of contact and comparison between the religions of the East and that of Jesus, as I gathered them by my own personal study and observation.

"It is natural for man to be religious. It was born in him. He breathed it with the breath of life. Away back in the mystic ages, at the very birth of

human intellect, we find men impressed
with the belief in the existence of a
divine principle, power or being, or in
other words, the belief in the existence
of a God, and to whom he sustained the
relationship of dependence, obligation
and hope.

" To the primitive man with untrained
mind, surrounded by dangers and diffi-
culties that he could not control, by the
various phenomena of nature that were
to him inscrutable, it is not strange
that he should feel his insignificance, his
helplessness, his dependence upon the
Supreme Power, and be moved to reverence, to worship, to curiosity and hope.

" Their idea of a God was, however,
very crude and vague; as time rolled
on and the mind began to develop, their
means of observation to increase, the
power of abstraction and generalization
began to appear. He was given a person and personalities, functions and
attributes, very similar often times to

their own peculiar ideas and passions,
until we find even at an early date, the
Divine principle completely covered up
with all manner of theories, ologies and
isms, more or less mysterious, corrupt
and complex. And at this later date
we have all manners of religions, more
or less surrounded by the mystical superstitions of the primitive mind, mis-
conceived, distorted, and misapplied by
speculative philosophers and dogmatical
religions. For a people living under
different and various circumstances and
environments, such as climatic influence,
different degrees of intellectuality, moral
accountability, and political government,
it would seem not an easy if a possible
thing to formulate a religion that would
meet all of the special demands and
needs peculiar to each branch or nation
of the people.

"God has given to no one people, to
no one nation, to no one religion, a
monopoly of the truth, and how errone-

ous for any one religion to gather about
itself the mantle of self-righteousness,
and cry out in a voice of scornful intolerance to all the other religions : ' You
are heathens, you are sinners, you are
in the wrong! Lo, here is the only
true religion ; come, and learn of me.'
As to the probabilities of a universal
religion in the future, it is hardly safe
to speculate. We have much to hope
from evolution and progress, but I
doubt if at any time will the world ever
as one people know any other universal
redeemer than God himself. 'Who at
divers times and in sundry manner
spake unto the fathers, has in these last
days spoken unto us by the Son?' To
the student of comparative theology, as
he turns over the pages of the books of
religions and reads with impartial mind,
there can be but little doubt as to how
many and who are the spiritual fathers
through whom God has spoken to each
nation of this people.

"To my old friend and teacher, Max
Muller. I am indebted for this axiom:
'He who knows but one religion knows
none,' the truth of which is at once apparent and impressive. To know a
religion one must be enabled to get
away from himself and look at it
through the eyes of the people by
whom it is professed. He must know
their language, and become acquainted
with their manners and customs, must
feel the influences that surround and
control their lives, must know the superstitions and traditions of their fathers, and look with impartial eyes and
honest purpose upon the seeking of his
fellow-men after God. When, having
learned of all religions, let him bring
home the golden truths he has found
and as searchlights use them in study-
ing the religion that God has sent him.

"As to the idea of Jesus having visited the countries of the Orient, from
the time of his disappearence from his-

tory until he began his ministry in
Judea, I have to say, that as far as I
have been able to discover, there is
abundant evidence in proof of such a
statement other than the many striking
similarities between his teaching and
those of the religions of the East, especially those of Gautama, the great In-
dian teacher, whose religion is the
religion of near five hundred millions of
people.

"In the time of Jesus there was sufficient means by which the Oriental
doctrines of religion could have reached
Palestine. As early as the third century before Christ, we know that there
was a well established commercial rela-
tion between the East and the countries
of the Mediterranean by which the pearl
and the gold of the land of Ophir found
its way into Palestine and the Bible
lands. Again we read that, during the
reign of Asoka, king of India three
centuries before Christ, a council of at

least a thousand religious scholars was convened at Patna. At Asoka's command, who was of the Buddhist faith, the proceedings of this council were engraven on the rocks and scattered about through the whole land of India. The Buddhists were great propagandists, and many missionaries were sent out to preach the religion of their beloved teacher, across the Himalayas, into the far off Asia and the surrounding isles. Strange if these zealous missionaries neglected the land of Palestine, but we have no word that such was or was not the case. I prefer to believe that what Jesus knew of the religions of the East, that he journeyed thither by caravans and studied them personally in the land where they were best known and revered.

"In the religion of Jesus there is so little that is new and so much that originally belonged to the great teachers who went before him, that the scholar who reads with a knowledge of Oriental literature must surely see at times that which will lead him to regard the Bible of the West as but a new version of the Bibles of the East.

" Zoroaster, many hundred, perhaps a thousand, years before Jesus trod this earth, taught a religion that believed in the existence of a supreme God, 'the Creator of the earthly and spiritual life,' 'the Lord of the whole universe, at whose hands are all the creatures of this world,' 'and whose promise unto those who believe in Him is everlasting life;' 'who showed the sun and the stars their way,' 'who caused the moon to wax and wane,' 'who holds the earth and skies above it,' 'who is in the wind and in the storm,' 'who grants to the pious who are pure in thought, in word and deed the reward of eternal life, and to the wicked eternal punishment.'

"The cultivation of truth, purity, obedience, temperance and industry are indeed the foundation stones of the religion of Zoroaster. 'Purity.' said he, 'is the best thing for a man after birth, and good thoughts, good works, good deeds are a safe guide to the gates of paradise.' The Zoroasterian practice of passing consecrated bread and a cup of soma wine to the worshipers bears a striking outward resemblance to the Lord's supper. The disciples of this sect were also taught that the washing in pure water was an essential factor in cleansing their bodies of moral and spiritual uncleanliness, as was that of prayer. The rite of the New Testament — baptism — is, however, of ancient Essenian origin.

"At least five hundred years before Christ, the great religionist of the Flowery Land gave to the world that leading principle of law known as the Golden Rule. Said Lao-tsze, 'Recompense injury with kindness,' and Confucius in the same great age gave it in the words,

'Do not unto others whatever ye would not that others should do unto you.'

"He also laid great stress on what are known to his followers as the five constants, viz., benevolence, wisdom, righteousness, worship, faithfulness. 'Those,' said he, 'who multiply good deeds will have joys running over, those who multiply evil deeds calamities to overflowing.' 'Honor thy father and thy mother,' was the most forcibly taught by Confucius in his rules to social life. The Logos idea is from neo-platonism, and the martyr Justin affirms that the 'Logos had worked through Socrates as it had been present in Jesus,' and also tells us that the seed of the Logos was 'implanted in every race.'

"The doctrine of the Trinity or Unity in one is of very ancient origin. Lao-tsze puts it thusly, 'Two in one and three in two,' but his disciples say, 'Three pure ones in trinity,' and Confucius talked of the 'absorption of the trinity in the finite.' Buddha puts it, 'One in union and three in division.'

"The doctrine of the atonement, or the deliverance of many by the virtues of one, though somewhat crude and mysterious, was known to all antiquity, as were the doctrines of reward and punishment for deeds done in this life.

"Of death, Confucius taught that, 'When flesh and bones die, the material becomes dust, but the immaterial rises above the grave in great light, has odor and is very pitiable. This same,' he says, 'though unseen, still continues to influence the lives of those in this world for many generations, or, in the words of our religion, they rest from their labors and their works to live after them.'

"'Love thy neighbor as thyself,' has an original in 'look upon all as upon your ownself,' of Ancient Advatia.

"The idea of worshiping God through love came from the Vedas of the ancient Hindus. In one of its many hymns we

find him spoken of as the 'one beloved.
more dear than anything in this or in
the next world.' 'It is good to love
God for the hope of reward, but better
to love Him for the sake of love.'

"Again, from the same source we are
told that as a 'lotus leaf grows in the
water and never is wet by the water, so
should the man live in this world, with his
heart to God and hand to work.' Here
we find the same thought as expressed
by Jesus in his saying, 'Let not the right
hand know what the left hand doeth,'
and many others of similar character.

"How familiar are these words taken
from one of the most ancient of Hindu
books, known as the Laws of Manu,
written probably nine hundred years
before Christ: 'And for whatever purpose a man bestows a gift, for a similar
purpose he shall receive a like reward.'

"'Let not a man be proud of his
righteous devotions, let him not having
sacrificed, utter a falsehood.'

"'Having made a donation. let him not proclaim it abroad.'

"' By falsehood the sacrifice becomes vain. by pride the merit of devotion is lost. and by proclaiming its largeness its fruit is destroyed. For. in his passage to the next world. neither his father. nor his mother. nor his wife. nor his son, nor any of his kinsmen accompany him.'

"'Single each man is born ; single he dies ; single he receives his reward of his good. and single the punishment of his evil deeds.'

"But the most striking similarities are, however. found in the religion of Gautama. who six centuries before the man of Galilee, appeared in Palestine, went with his band of disciples through the whole land of India preaching the law of holiness to his fellow-man. It is said that during his ministry of forty-five years he preached not less than eighty-four thousand sermons, and was familiar with doctrines of eighty-two religious creeds or sects. In the character and religion of Buddha there is so much of charity, love and compassion for his fellow-beings, so much of tolerance, patience, self-denial and all lovable attributes, that one cannot become acquainted with his religion and history without a feeling of the greatest love and veneration. Though wrapped about with complex metaphysics and tedious narrations and ancient legends of the East, it is not difficult for the student to trace in his teachings an inspiration that is Divine. Nor to see truly as the Hindu Krishna exclaimed, 'God is in every religion like unto a thread running through a string of pearls. And when thou seest extraordinary holiness connected to extraordinary power, raising the purity of mankind, know ye that God is there.'

"Nowhere in all my travels have I ever met with so kind, so gentle, so hospitable or tolerant a people as are the Buddhists. It is a part of their religious duty to be hospitable to strangers, to take care of the sick and the needy, and to exercise great patience and tolerance for the religions of all people.

"As far as human suffering is concerned the records of Buddha are stainless. They tell of no holy wars: no inquisition; no burning of heretics, or witches, or scholars, nor banishment of unbelievers from their native land. Their conquests were all made without persecution or bloodshed.

"In teaching the peace of man and his salvation, Buddhism appeals to the rational mind of man and the better impulses of the human heart. Shall not we give them the honor due them for their religion that has made them so mild, though not without its errors and superstitions, its symbols and relics, its beads and bells, its monasteries and shrines, its pilgrimages and processions, its

candles and incense, its robes and idols,
shall not we, who make use of many of
the same symbols and ceremonies in the
worship of our God, and look upon it
all as but the visible means of worship
and not the being worshiped, shall not
we extend to them our sympathy, our
tolerance and our charity. The Saint
Josaphat of the Catholic Church is no
doubt none other than the loved Buddha of India. When Buddaa came into
this world he saw what Zoroaster saw,
saw what Confucius saw, saw what Jesus
saw, saw what we see to-day — human
misery, human sorrow, human suffering
and sin. All life, the very earth seemed
to him to be loaded down with an ever-
present ever-changing cycle of human
suffering. His great, tender, loving
heart was filled with compassion for his
fellow - sufferers. He would that he
might relieve them from this bondage.
I need not recount to you the story of
his birth, nor give you the details of his

severe discipline, the self-mortification, and the long stages of contemplation, through which he passed before he arrived at the solution of the problem of human pain and misery. How at last it came to him, when sitting beneath the spreading boughs of a bo tree, that *ignorance* was the cause of it all, and finally a little later on that *truth* was the great emancipator.

"'All suffering,' said he, 'arises from ignorance. You shall know the truth and the truth shall set you on fire.'

"Both Buddha and Jesus were of royal birth, and both were hailed while yet in early infancy by the saint and the sage as the savior of the world and the king of kings.

"Both came near being put to death by the hands of a zealous monarch, who saw in each a possible rival for his throne. Both excelled their teachers in wisdom and learning. Buddha, it is said, could talk from the day of his birth, and

and while yet a child explained the
names of sixty-four alphabets to his
teacher, as did the child Jesus explain
to his teacher the meaning of the Hebrew alphabet.

" Both tried a life of asceticism and
carried their fasts to the extreme. Buddha had an encounter with Mara the
Prince of Darkness, through whom he
underwent a stormy temptation before
he gained the final victory over self and
the passions of worldly life.

" Jesus was tempted by the devil.
Both wandered about homeless and
penniless, dependent entirely upon the
charity of the people. To both are attri-
buted the performance of many miracles.
Of both we read that they officiated in
a miraculous way at the marriage feast,
Buddha causing a small amount of food
to feed an astonishingly great number
of wedding guests.

" Both were powerful teachers, and
preached to all classes of people alike.

Both possessed an extraordinary influence over the minds of men, both by the peculiar earnestness and purity of their teachings and the compassionate, sympathetic qualities of their personalities. Both were given to teaching by the way of parables, many of which are drawn from the same sources. There is the parable of the lost son, the worldly fool, the sower, the mustard seed, etc.

"Both Buddha and Jesus gathered about them a band of disciples, one of each being the best beloved. Aranda was the favorite of Buddha, as John was the favorite of Jesus. Both sent their disciples out into the world to proclaim the gospel of peace and love to all humanity. Said Buddha to his disciples when he sent them out: 'Go ye and wander forth for the gain of many, in compassion for the world, for the good, for the gain and welfare of gods and man. Let not two of you go the same way. Proclaim the doctrine glorious. Preach ye a life of perfect, pure holiness. Go into every country and convert those not converted. Go, filled with compassion, to the rescue and to save. Proclaim that a blessed Buddha has appeared in the world, and that he is preaching the law of holiness.'

"'Like a chain of blind men,' said Buddha, 'is the discourse of the Brahmans; he that is in front sees nothing, he that is behind sees nothing. he that is in the middle sees nothing. What then? Is not the faith of the Brahmans in vain?'

"In similar manner Jesus. speaking of the Pharisees, likened them unto the 'blind leading the blind.'

"Said Buddha, 'If ye are unhappy in this world, it is because of past sins.'

"'Whatsoever a man soweth, that shall he also reap,' is the way Jesus gave utterance to the same truth.

"'Come unto me and I will give you peace,' said Buddha; 'come unto me and I will give you rest.' 'Peace I leave with you, my peace I give unto you.' said Jesus.

"'It is difficult for the rich and the noble to be religious.' said Buddha. 'It is easier for the camel to go through the needle's eye.' said Jesus, 'than for a rich man to enter into the kingdom of Heaven.'

"'Better far with red-hot irons put out both your eyes. than to encourage in yourselves lustful thoughts,' said Buddha. 'If thy right eye offend thee, pluck it out.' said Jesus.

"'At certain times and places somehow do leaders appear in the world, just as the blossom of the glomerous fig tree is rare, also beautiful and far more wonderful is the law I proclaim,' said Buddha. It is a strange coincidence that Jesus should make use of the same symbol in speaking of the signs of the coming of the Son of Man.

"How curiously familiar are these Buddhistic passages. I need not repeat their similarities.

"'Take then the bow of earnest perseverance and the sharp arrow point of wisdom.'

"'Cover your heads with a helmet of good thoughts and fight with fixed purpose against the five desires.'

"'He who turns his pound into five will be set over five cities: he who turns it into ten, over ten cities.' 'Touch not a woman's hand with corrupt thoughts.' 'Commit no adultery.'

"'What men call treasures, when laid up in a deep pit profit nothing and may easily be lost, but the real treasure is that laid up by man or woman through charity, piety and self-control.' 'Let us live happily together, not hating those that hate us; let us live free from hatred among men.' 'He that observes the law and is compassionate is my disciple.'

"'Look not to any one for a refuge beside yourselves.'

"'Let man overcome anger by kindness, evil by good.'

"'My law is a law of grace for man.'

"'Be ye lamps to yourselves.'

"'Neither abstinence from eating, nor going naked, nor shaving the head, nor diet, nor rough garments, nor sacrifice will cleanse a man from his delusion.'

"'Fools follow after vanity, the man of sense after wisdom.'

"'To abhor and cease from sin, abstinence from strong drink, not to be weary in well-doing. Reverence and lowliness, contentment and gratitude, the hearing of the law at due season, to be long-suffering and meek, is the greatest blessing.'

"'Strive on and thou shall soon be free from impurities.'

"In almost the very same words of our religion Buddha taught that we should love our neighbor as ourselves;

and enjoined upon the rich that they should devote one-fourth of their abundance to the poor. Virtue is frequently compared to living waters, and religion to the pearl and jewels. 'It is also,' said he, 'like the salt of the ocean, one in taste throughout.' 'Do not let it fall into the hands of fools.' The world he compared to a city of sand. 'Its foundations cannot endure.'

"Let me give you Buddha's ten commandments very briefly:

"'Do not destroy life. Do not steal. Do not commit adultery. Do not tell a falsehood. Do not speak evil of others. Do not be greedy. Do not indulge in intoxicating drinks. Do not be cruel. Do not indulge in passions. Do not be intolerant and uncharitable.'

"Another strange similarity that is strikingly pathetic is the last words of these divine teachers. 'Everything that cometh into being passeth away,' said Buddha, as he passed peacefully away

in the arms of his best beloved disciple,
Aranda; but how sadly different were
the surroundings from which came the
death-cry of Jesus as he hung upon the
Roman cross: 'It is finished.'

"It is said that Buddhism knows no God,
no existence for the soul after death.

"Buddha's teaching was more for the
man of this world than the world to
come. His religion is to show man
how to become perfect in this life, or to
attain and enjoy Nirvana, the state of
peaceful tranquillity, on this earth. I do
not believe that Nirvana means utter
annihilation of the soul, but rather utter
annihilation of the body, its passions,
its evil dispositions, through which the
soul becomes at peace or rest with the
world and his fellow man.

"If Buddha believed this state of
Nirvana to mean utter annihilation, why
do the Buddhists pray to him? If there
is no God, no Buddha, why is this
prayer? Why pray at all?

"'Thou, Buddha, victor over the hosts of evil, thou all-wise being, come down to our world, made perfect and glorified by bygone evolutions; always pitiful, always gentle towards all creatures; look down upon us, for the time is come to pour out thy blessing upon the people. Be gracious to us from thy throne built in the heaven. Thou art the eternal redeemer of all creatures, therefore bow down to us with all thy unstained heavenly societies.'

"In accounting for the similarities in the teaching of Buddha and Jesus, only a few of which I have given, I cannot but believe that force of conditions and the circumstances account satisfactorily for it all. In some way or other Jesus must have come in contact with the religion of Buddha and noted its influence for good to humanity.

"Another singularity in the history of these two religions, and what may be regarded as the connecting link, is the

12

fact that Buddha foretold of the coming of a Buddha who would be called Maitreya, or the teacher of love. May it not be that his prophecy had reference to Jesus of Galilee? May it not be that his mission was to complete the works of Buddha, or was he a re-incarnation of the great teacher? The answer is yet to come from the ages yet to be.

"In conclusion, gentlemen, I freely admit there is no positive proof that Jesus was in the East during his absence from Palestine. As he astounded his teachers at the age of twelve, it is improbable that he was idle mentally during the following eighteen years, and there is such a chain of circumstantial evidence that he did spend the time in oriental countries, that I have no doubt upon the subject.

"It is not denied by any scholar that a similarity of belief, and inventions and the conduct of the people remote from each other is no evidence *per se* of

intercommunication. The evidence fur-
nished by the ages of stone, bone, iron
and bronze having extended over the
world is a demonstration that a certain
stage of mental development produces
a similarity in conduct among people
never having had any knowledge of
each other.

"It is also true that men in different
nations, remote from each other, appear
to be merely a mouthpiece or instru-
ment through whom the same thoughts
or beliefs burst forth, and the beliefs or
discoveries are simply concomitants. .
The discovery of the planet Uranus by
Levarier of France and Adams of England is a striking example, but when
there is a striking similarity of the
teaching throughout the lives of two or
more individuals — nay, almost *absolute
sameness* — other than natural causes
must be sought for in explanation.
There was absolutely nothing taught by
Jesus that had not been taught cen-

turies before by Zoroaster, Confucius
and Gautama, *and in almost the same
words; the same parables were used, and
the same allegories.* The Buddhists' *ten*
commandments are in almost the identi-
cal language of those given by Moses,
and the Sermon on the Mount by Confucius and Gautama have in them
substantially the same language found
in the Sermon on the Mount by Jesus.

"The commercial relations subsisting
between India and Palestine would not
have brought the savants learned in
theological lore, but men interested in
the material things of life. Jesus'
knowledge of the teachings in the East
must have required years to obtain it.
It was acquired during his long absence
from Palestine, in India. I believe future investigation will demonstrate it.

"Zoroaster, Confucius, Buddha and
Jesus were alike able to interpret the
language of a tear, and hear the voice
of a groan."

CHAPTER IX.

NO IDLE PHANTOM.

Soon the noise and bustle of breaking camp became evident, and with the marching order of that day began that memorable countermarch of over three hundred miles. March, march, march, onward they press, still onward, toward the north and home.

The rest was of short duration. Hood made a flank movement, and his army pushed to the north of Atlanta, in the neighborhood of Rome, Georgia. Of the movements of Sherman's army, his pursuit and his unsuccessful effort to force the Confederate army to battle, the division of the Union army and his march to the sea with the larger part of it are matters of history. Hood's objective point was far to the north, perhaps Nashville, or even further north.

Less than two corps of Sherman's entire
army were left to follow, or be followed
by the Confederate army. Hood in his
march north made a desperate but unsuccessful attempt to carry Altoona
Pass by storm, then held and commanded by one of Iowa's bravest men,
Gen. John M. Corse. The generalship
displayed by Corse, and the gallantry by
his men on that occasion was not sur-
passed during the war.

Their feet tread the same paths as
they retrace the scenes of their recent
victories. They recross the battle-
fields where so lately the ground was
stained with the lifeblood of their com-
panions, and where the thousands of
nameless graves tell pitiful tales of
widowed hearts, of fatherless children,
of mothers' longing arms, of vacant
chairs at home.

The indifference of the soldiers at
that time is something almost incomprehensible. They made no moan over the

loss of comrades, sought out no graves, shed no tears. Their actions and words attested their indifference to death on either side.

On one occasion as they camped on the site of one of the battles of a few weeks before, a sturdy-looking soldier, with a bullet-hole in his hat, pointed to a single tree that stood a few rods to his left, and with a look that betrayed no feeling, scarcely even interest, remarked, "There is just where I stood when I sent that rebel major to the front parlor of the New Jerusalem with his boots and spurs."

Viewed from the age of patriotic enthusiasm, we wonder their hearts did not burst with pent-up feeling, or that their thirst for vengeance had not overstepped all bounds and resorted to the atrocities of barbarous nations.

As they passed the point in the line of battle about Kenesaw mountain, occupied by his division when that disas-

trous charge was made a few weeks
before. Wallace removed his hat, and
said to Colonel Dale, as they rode forward : "Here is where so many of my
boys answered to the last roll-call, and
are now at parade rest. They have
passed from the strife and conflict of
earthly life and rebel shot and shell to
the quiet scenes beyond the cold surges
of the mystic river. No more shall
reveille or battle disturb their repose.
In the serenity of death they won everlasting victory. Heaven's doors stood
wide open."

The army halted for dinner near a
beautiful spring that poured out of the
hillside. A log house, minus much of
the "chinking and dobing," and the
roof having the appearance of having
seen better days, stood near to it in a
clearing of about fifteen acres of land,
situated on a steep hillside, surrounded
by a rail fence that gave evidence of the
camp fires by both Union and Confeder-

ate armies. As Wallace and his staff
rode up to ask about the missing gourd
at the spring, a typical southerner of
about sixty-five years emerged from the
shanty. He wore a gray suit, that
would have been improved by several
Cleveland badges, a slouch hat with a
broad brim, and a pair of cow-hide
boots with ample means of ventilation,
into which his pantlegs were tucked.
Both his unsocked great toes were
plainly visible. His hair was long and
cut square; his beard had the beauty
and simplicity of nature untouched; his
shirt was open far down for want of
buttons: his pants were cut barn-door
fashion, and the button on one side
necessary to retain the flap in position,
was absent. Two crippled horses, left
by the Confederate cavalry, limped up
the hillside, and a cow that was no
temptation, even to soldiers living on
short rations of salt meat, was tied to
an old wagon without a bed. He said,

as he squirted a mouthful of tobacco
juice over the bare heads of four or five
of his children that had followed him out
of the house,—a part of it remaining
on his mustache and beard, — " Well,
Gineral, youens is here agin."

" Yes," said Wallace, "and I suppose
you are glad to see us. You are a
Union man?"

"Yes, Gineral, I am a good Union
man. I told the old woman just yester-
that youens had treated us a derned
sight better than wenns had. You see,
Gineral, I am not what the college chaps
call educated. I can't read nor write,
but the old woman says nater did a
power for me, and she's a purty good,
sound thinker, I tell you. You see, I
catch onto things right smart. I heard
Gineral Jackson say, ni' twenty years
ago, that a wise man could change his
mind when it was necessary, but a fool
couldn't do it at all. When Johnson's
army passed here, I didn't think as I do

now. Yes, Gineral, I am solid for the
Union."

"You seem to be pretty well fixed,
and to be happy and contented," said
Wallace.

" Yes, Gineral," he said. "I came here
thirty years ago a poor man. Me and
the old woman has worked hard, *and we
have saved what we made.* 'Pears to me
nearly everybody makes lots of money,
but the p'int is, they don't save it. All
you see, Gineral, is mine, and it's paid
for, too ;" and, taking another chew of
tobacco, he continued with a knowing
smile, "it hain't ornamented with a
mortgage. e'ther."

"Have you a large plantation?" said
Wallace.

"Yes, Gineral, purty large — about
thirty acres, but I got it by industry.
I have not been out of the county since
I came here, and I have only been to
Cassville, seven miles, once in fifteen
years."

"Are there any Unitarians in this neighborhood?" said Wallace.

"I don't know, sah; I never seed any; but some varmint has carried off what few chickens we had left after Johnson's army passed through, and, if they like chickens, I reckon that's where they have gone."

The chaplain had ridden up in time to hear what the planter said, and he, in a grave and serious manner, said: "My dear sir, I know all about Unitarians; they have infested the state in which I live for years, and I say to you they are awfully dangerous. They are even more to be dreaded on account of your children than your chickens, *and they are alarmingly fond of chickens.*"

"Be they big varmints?" said the planter.

"*Big!*" said the chaplain, "I saw one not a mile back in the timber that would weigh two hundred pounds dressed."

The old man looked around to see if

any of the children were gone, and, as
he squirted a mouthful of tobacco juice,
part of which fell on Wallace's boots,
said nervously, "Lord, children, run to
your mother."

Slowly but steadily the army pressed
on till the days grew into weeks and the
weary weeks dragged on to months.
No battles, no skirmishes, no opposition
of any description broke the monotony
of their long tramp. They almost
longed for the smell of powder, the
roar of the artillery, the crash of the
musketry. But though Hood's army
moved northward at the same time,
almost parallel with our line of march,
and at a distance of from ten to fifty
miles, our troops sought no encounter,
for his men numbered three to our
one.

The fare was poor and the men
showed little relish for their daily rations of bacon, beans and hardtack.
Not a few sickened and died.

Just as the shades of evening began to fall between the day and the night the army pitched its tents and bivouacked for the night in a clearing from which the bridge three miles south of Resaca was plainly visible. Wallace and Dale without the interchange of a word, but as if impelled by the same invisible forces, walked together in the direction of the bridge.

In the mind of each were visions of the vast difference in the effects of an action done or left undone. Thoughts of all the brave men who had gone down to death during the late campaign surged over Wallace. A feeling of superstition, of something uncanny, of something almost supernatural, oppressed him. He knit his brows, drew himself to his full height and shrugged his shoulders as something very like a shudder passed over him. In vain he sought to dispel this feeling, to cast it aside as something unworthy.

At length he spoke. "Is your mind also beset, Dick, with doubts, as you gaze at yonder bridge? Does there come to you the haunting image of what might have been the issue if it had been burned, cutting off Johnson's supplies and his means of escape? True, he would probably have thrown his whole force on our division, but even had we been completely annihilated the cost would have been so infinitely small compared to the price that has been paid in human lives.

"The brightest of those lives that has gone out forever on this earth still casts a radiance that will illuminate all time to come, and leaves a halo round the name of General McPherson.

"How gladly would I exchange my lot for his! How gladly give him back to earth, to life, and in his stead lie camly down to sleep the sleep of death; and then, perchance to wake where Agnes waits, and hand in hand with her

live on through all eternity!" Unshed
tears glistened in his eyes and his strong
form trembled with emotion as he continued: "I know it is not far to where
she waits, for day by day I feel her
presence; I feel her guiding hand and
her protecting influence. Before each
battle, aye, on the very field of battle,
this feeling is so strong within me that
her name springs involuntarily to my
lips. Dick, oh, Dick, is this a phantom
of my brain, or is the veil so thin between this life and the next that love
can pierce its film and hold communion
with the soul? Is she my guardian
angel?"

Overcome with agitation, his voice
choked with sobs; Dale extended his
hand to his friend as he exclaimed, "It is
no idle phantom; surely, surely, you two
stand soul to soul and heart to heart."

At daybreak the following morning
the camp was astir with preparations
for continuing the march.

After a march of three miles the army reached Resaca, and here occurred one of those pleasant things which history, intent upon the outcome of a struggle, ignores as unimportant. But to those fifteen thousand ill-fed men it was no little thing. It filled a long felt want, it touched a vital spot. There were situated in this town seven bakeries, and when news reached there that the steady tramp, tramp of the nation's heroes would bring them to that immediate vicinity, each of these bakeries must have carried on operations to the utmost extent of its capacity, for upon the arrival of the army every man became the sole possessor of a loaf of baker's bread. The rejoicing of these men over a single loaf of bread was something pathetic. Great, rough, brawny men and delicate, pale-faced boys marched on side by side, bearing their precious burdens, laughing, singing, shouting. On they marched into the depth of the forest,

that thickly wooded tract that stretched
almost the length of the hundreds of
miles that lay between them and Columbia. Tennessee.

The only sounds were the resounding
echo of that mighty condensed tread
and the startled notes of the sweet wild
birds.

CHAPTER X

LATE in November the Union army, consisting of two depleted corps, with a less fighting force than 14,000, confronted General Hood and his army of more than 55,000 fighting men at Columbia, Tennessee. General Schofield, who was the ranking general, had been compelled to leave the city and cross the river late in the afternoon. We then believed, and I now believe, Hood had misled Schofield as to the point at which he intended to cross the river. A small Union force had been sent up the river to prevent his crossing at that point. That force was intercepted by Hood's army, and did not participate in the battle at Franklin two days later, but were compelled to cross the Tennessee river and come to the army at

Nashvile ten days later. Whether any blunder was made in sending a force to that point where Hood did not cross nor attempt to cross, future history will determine. Hood crossed the river two miles below, and at or about the time Schofield crossed at Columbia. Several Confederate batteries were hurried into Columbia as soon as it was evacuated by the Union forces; for the shelling continued from that side of the river until we were out of range of their guns.

When a half a mile from the river, General Wallace was taking a careful survey of the Confederate batteries with his glass, and his orderly was standing near him. A solid shot from one of the Confederate guns struck the ground about twenty rods from where they stood; it ricochetted, and on its upward motion struck the orderly on the side of his head and took it off down to his lower jaw. The General's clothing was spotted with blood and brain. With tears in his eyes, the General said: "A strange fatality comes to my orderlies; this is five I have had killed in battle. That shot, however, was intended for me."

The march for Spring Hill, situated midway between Columbia and Franklin, and ten miles from either, was begun. When about three or four miles on the way, General Wallace sent an order to Colonel Dale, who had command of his regiment, to go back and guard a cross-road leading over to the stone pike, running almost parallel with the one on which the Union army was moving.

The road was soon found and a strong picket line established. Within an hour after the pickets were on duty our entire army, wagon train, ambulances and ordnance had passed; the only sound to be heard was the rumbling made by Hood's army, less than two miles to our right, on the stone pike leading to

Spring Hill. After an hour Hood's entire army had passed, and no sound was heard; the stillness was painful. The entire regiment except the pickets, Colonel Dale and myself, slept as soundly as if they had been at home. The Colonel and I walked back and forth along the pike, expecting to be captured by the Confederate cavalry, if he did not receive order soon relieving him from duty at that point. No order came. He was not known to be nervous during his army life except on that occasion.

He said: "I fear the Confederate cavalry are now between us and our command, but I dare not leave this place without orders, especially so as it was General Wallace who gave me the order to guard this road."

After an hour's consultation, he determined that an order relieving him had probably been sent, and that the messenger had encountered the Confeder-

ate cavalry and had been killed. We
learned from Wallace, the next day,
that such an order was sent, but it was
not received and the messenger is
among the "missing."

The regiment was waked, the pickets
called in, and in a few minutes we were
marching at a rapid pace toward Spring
Hill. Every man then appeared to appreciate the situation. Our own command at least six miles away, and it was
probable that Hood's army was in camp
covering our road. We had gone less
than two miles when we were fired on
by cavalry in our front. The regiment
was deployed in line of battle. The
command to charge was given by Dale
in a shrill tone that rang through the
forest, and its echo came back two distinct times, followed by a roll of musketry that I seem to hear yet. A volley
at night is very different from a volley
in the day. The cavalry disappeared,
the march was resumed and no other

obstacle was found in our way. We reached Spring Hill at 2 o'clock in the morning.

When we came in sight, there appeared to our right what appeared to me like ten thousand camp-fires, extending up to within twenty rods of the road on which we were marching. We did not know whether they were Union or Confederate soldiers, and we came near going straight to them when we came to Spring Hill, which I suppose had in it thirty or forty houses. The night was dark; our infantry was asleep lying along the road: the wagon train, ambulances and artillery were mixed in such a confusion that an attack by Hood at that time would certainly have been disastrous.

We did not find General Wallace that night, but continued our march until we were at the head of the column. When orders to move were given, we were in the front, and we were the first into

Franklin about 8 o'clock the next morning. We at that time believed General Cleburne cried because Hood would not give the order for a night attack. I have heard in the last year that Hood gave the order and it was not executed. What the facts were may never be known, as General Cleburne and nine other Confederate generals were killed the next day at the battle of Franklin.

General Wallace and his command arrived about an hour later, at 9 o'clock, and Colonel Dale reported to him in person, expecting a reprimand, or even more severe punishment, for disobeying his orders.

The General took both of his hands and said: "Colonel Dale, God bless you. I am so glad to see you. I have been in torture all night, fearing you had fallen into the hands of the enemy, or even something worse."

"But, General, I disobeyed orders, and the order was in your handwriting, and it was because it was *your order* that I dreaded so much to disobey it."

"Colonel. you have never disobeyed an order in your life. It was hastily written and was imperfect : it ought to have said. ' You are relieved when the entire command has passed.' You simply supplemented the order with your own good judgment. The awful danger to which you and that regiment were exposed almost unnerves me now. I know, rather than to have been captured. you would have fought Hood's entire army. with the inevitable result of every man having been killed. Why. even before the last of our column had reached Spring Hill. the Confederate camp-fires extended from a point not thirty rods from our road. a mile away ; and the Colonel of the 124th Indiana regiment rode up within speaking distance of the camp-fire and said, ' What regiment is this?' The answer came, ' What's left of the 36th Alabama.'

"I am glad to see you; first, for your own safety, and second, we shall need you before the sun goes down. Mark my words, Hood is going to play for great stakes to-day. He has three men to our one, the river is somewhat swollen, the bridge is gone, and we have not time to pontoon it and cross before he is upon us. *We shall have to fight him right here, and before night.* Hood and his army have the strongest inducements held out to them to do deeds of daring presented during the war. If our army is crushed and captured, Hood will be in Nashville to-morrow, the next day in Louisville, and he can then march over Indiana and Ohio at his pleasure. Sherman is on his way to 'the sea.' Grant has need of his entire army. If, therefore, Hood is successful to-day, there is absolutely no barrier to his spreading desolation over the North. Over and above even that, Hood is personally ambitious. If he wins and

invades the North, his reputation as a
general is established.

" You will personally superintend the
construction of the entire line of breast-
works to be occupied by my command.
See that they are as good as they can be
made. Have a trench dug wide enough,
at the most exposed points of the line,
for two or three men to stand in, so that
those in the rear can load while the
front line does the firing." Before 2
o'clock the entire command had arrived,
and fairly good breast-works were completed, extending from the river above
to the river below, a distance of about
three - fourths of a mile, embracing
Franklin in a semi-circle. Both officers and men in Hood's entire army were
confident of victory, and their enthusiasm was wrought to the highest point.
Even the intrepid and scholarly Cleburne said to General Hood that day
that he " never had so much confidence
in the ultimate success of our cause."

They were promised new clothing, equipments of all kinds, and army supplies that were stored in Nashville. Hood was jubilant; he was confident that he would either capture us or drive us into the river.

Two of our brigades were stationed in line of battle about fifteen hundred feet in advance of our main line, and they had thrown up very light earth-works. General Wallace remonstrated against any force whatever in front of our line of battle, not even a picket line was necessary, much less two brigades; there was nothing to obstruct the view. We can see when the charge begins, if it is a mile away, and whatever force is in front of our main line will be swept back with, or just before, the advancing Confederate line of battle, and may delay the firing by our men, or endanger the lives of our own men.

A little after 2 o'clock indications of the approaching battle were seen by the movements of Hood's army a mile distant. The waving of signal-flags, and soon thereafter the formation of the line of battle. About 4 o'clock in the afternoon their lines moved forward in splendid order, as if on dress parade, their colors floating in the breeze, and their arms at right-shoulder shift. As they approached our skirmish line the Confederate yell was heard all along the line: they struck the double quick and pressed forward with the determination of heroes. Our skirmish line was swept back on the two brigades; the brigade gave way and were hurled back on our main line in utter confusion. Our flying brigades, our skirmish line and the Confederate lines struck our fortification at the same time. The firing from our line of works was prevented by the approach of our own men. The charge was so impetuous that many Confederates fell headlong over the works and were bayonetted before they regained their feet.

A hand to hand conflict to death took place in the rear of out entrenchment. A superior Confederate force was overpowering our line; it wavered, and for a moment our works to the left of the center of our line was in Confederate hands. Those were awful moments. A yell of victory with increased desperation came from all along the Confederate line. At this moment General Wallace, General Stanley and Colonel Dale rode their horses right up to and into the fiercest part of the conflict, reformed the line and, with their swords, dealt death around them and drove the Confederates out of our entrenchments. General Stanley was shot from his horse just as the repulse was complete. They retired sullenly beyond the crest of the hill in our front and reformed their lines. Their loss had been very great. General Gordon was captured with over one thousand prisoners, and many battle flags. General Adams and his horse were killed while his horse was astride of our works. In a few minutes another desperate charge was made all along our line, and was repulsed with terrible slaughter.

Between 4 o'clock and midnight twelve charges were made, and were every time repulsed with heavy Confederate loss. I think it no exaggeration to say the most desperate fighting of the war was at the battle of Franklin. The Confederate generals led their men with great desperation and unsurpassed personal courage, and paid for their rashness with their lives. Here fell the Confederate Generals Scott, Quarrels, Strahl, Gist, Cochrell, Maninwault, Cleburne, Cranbury, and General Carter who fell from his horse mortally wounded and died within sight of his own house. He was found early next morning by his sister. The loss of the Confederate officers was so great that in several instances a captain was the ranking officer in a brigade. General Cleburne was killed in the second charge, while his horse was astride our works. The especially sad and tragic death of General Carter, within a few rods of his own palatial mansion, was regretted even by the Union soldiers.

By reference to the records, it will be found that the Confederate loss in killed and wounded in the battle of Frankin was greater in proportion to the number engaged than in any other battle of the late war. The rapid and precise firing of our men was not equaled in any other battle. They stood up three deep in the rifle-pits, and the rear ranks loaded while the front rank did the firing. The Confederate army lost in the battle of Franklin, in killed, wounded, prisoners and missing, about 13,000 men.

A calm and dispassionate reflection, after thirty years, upon the cause that led to victory and prevented defeat —

a defeat that would have been as deplorable as a defeat would have been at Gettysburg, and in the same way, of an invasion of the North by the Confederate army — was largely, if not wholly, due to the personal gallantry, and perhaps unequaled true heroism of General Wallace and Colonel Dale. General Schofield's headquarters, during the entire battle and before it begun, was at the fort on the other side of the river, a mile and a half distant. It is true General Stanley rode with Wallace and Dale into the most deadly part of the conflict, but he was early in the first charge shot in the neck and fell from his horse. In every one of the twelve separate and distinct charges made by the determined Confederate army, led by brave and reckless generals, they were in the saddles and as near the trench in the rear of the breastworks as it was possible to be. The unbounded confidence in General Wal-

lace by every soldier, the cool, steady
gaze of his great, blue eyes, his
earnest, kind words. "Stand firm, boys,
there is victory in the air." and his
imperial personage made him a tower of
strength.

The dashing valor of Colonel Dale —
he was where the line was most pressed,
wherever the bullets were the thickest,
there was seen his girlish, smiling
face, and it was always a talisman of
hope. That either of them survived
the battle seems to have been almost a
miracle. General Wallace had ten bullet marks in his clothing; one of his
shoulder-straps was shot away, there
were three holes through his hat, and
the rest were through his coat. Colonel
Dale had two bullet holes through his
hat, his sword-belt was cut in two by a
saber, and he lost the belt and the scab-
bard; his sword was knocked from his
hand by a bullet, but he dismounted and
got it again; three buttons were shot

off his coat. There were in all seventeen bullet marks and a saber cut in his clothing, without a scratch on his person. Before 2 o'clock in the morning our entire force had crossed the river, and on the evening of that day we were in Nashville.

"Good morning, General Wallace."

"Good morning, Mr. Calvin; come in."

"If it is not an intrusion, General, I would like to congratulate you upon your miraculous escape from the danger of the battle at Franklin."

"It is no intrusion; I am always glad to see my old chaplain, and here is Colonel Dale."

"You are both here because of God's protecting care, for which I have thanked Him in prayer, as I suppose you have both done. I had a splendid opportunity to see the awful grandeur of a battle with nothing but the smoke to obscure the view. In all the other battles I saw almost nothing for the heavy timber prevented a view of what was happening. except the movements very near to me. It is true at Pittsburg Landing and Chickamauga, at Stone River, and once or twice in the Atlanta campaign, I saw you begin a charge and nothing more, but at Franklin I saw it all, until the smoke became so dense that everything disappeared. The surgeons informed me that the temporary hospital would be at the church, directly in the rear of where you sat on your horse. I went into the belfry to be out of danger and to *watch a battle*. I saw the Confederate lines of battle formed a mile away. I saw them start; I saw them when they struck a double-quick, as you call it. It appeared to me like a careless trot, as if they were in a little hurry to get to a picnic. There were five distinct lines of battle, and they carried their guns at right shoulder shift until they were within two hundred yards of our works. Their anxiety and gait increased as they neared our line. I saw the impetuosity with which they would strike our works. Their officers were all mounted and almost in the line of battle, their swords blazing in the sun, their colors flying, and when the Confederate yell broke forth I trembled for the safety of our line. I saw you, General Stanley and Colonel Dale sitting unconcernedly on your horses, and I watched with breathless anxiety to see both batteries of six guns each, situated directly in your front, open fire. They were still as the graves, when it appeared to me they ought to be belching forth grape and canister upon the Confederate line rapidly approaching and now very near our works. I heard the crash, I felt the shock; the Confederate colors were planted on our breast-works; our line wavered and gave way. At a point in your front it appeared to me to be giving way on both sides of the center of our works, now actually in the Confederate hands. I closed my eyes, dreading the worst, and said, 'May God and Wallace prevent an utter rout.' When I opened them again, General Stanley was falling from his horse. You appeared collossal in size; your horse at the breast-works, your sword high above your head. I heard your words, 'Stand firm, boys, there is victory in the air.' I saw Colonel Dale have a hand-to-hand encounter with a mounted Confederate officer, whose horse was astride the breast-works. I have since learned the mounted officer who fell there was the gallant General Cleburne. At that moment the charge was repulsed. Your country owes you a debt of gratitude, which I hope it will repay in the future. It appears to me so apparent that the hand of God was your shield during that battle, and perhaps it was for the purpose of enabling you to see the all important doctrine of election and atonement as you have never seen them."

The general shook his head, smiled
and said : "Mr. Calvin, I am not conscious of any change upon those subjects, except it be a deeper conviction
that I am right and that you are wrong.
It appears to me that reason and
common sense must be wholly ignored
to enable any one to believe such palpa-
ble dogmas. You say a little sin is as
big as a big one, and that one little sin,
if unforgiven, will *forever* damn any
human soul. You also say, 'No man
lives without sin for one day.' Now,
Mr. Chaplain, if all men, yourself in-
cluded, sin every day, and if every sin
unforgiven will bring eternal perdition
to those having been guilty, suppose a
stray bullet were to kill you just after
one of those little sins, before you had
time for 'Godly sorrow '— whatever that
may mean — where would you establish
your headquarters? In hell or Heaven?
And what benefit could you derive from
'election,' and 'atonement,' and 'bap-

tism,' and the 'Lord's supper?' It will
not do, Mr. Chaplain: such sophistry
will not take the place of logic. We
both know, from personal observation
of men in the army and out of it, that
those making loud professions of piety
need watching: that they are no better
than those who go unostentatiously
about their own business. I do not believe all men sin every day. I now
know many men whom I believe have
not sinned while in the army, *unless being in the army is a sin*, which *is* true *if*
love of humanity is above love of country."

"General," said the chaplain, "your
opportunities have been great, and your
acquirements phenomenal in their scope
and in their profundity. There appears
to me, however, an indelible impress on
your mind of the instruction you received from Humboldt, Darwin and Max
Muller, which renders your mind icy
cold to everything except the truths of

mathematics, and the severest logic.
You are as yet, I fear a stranger to the
warm and devout faith, which has the
power of subordinating the head to
the heart. Notwithstanding your learning, you do not appear to me to comprehend man's sinful nature, and God's
desire to save him. The relationship
between God and man can be concisely
stated thus: Man stands guilty before
God. He has broken the laws of life.
Those laws entail an eternal penalty.
That penalty is death. That death,
however, means the dying out of the
spiritual nature while the intellectual
and physical natures live on forever in
hell. God wishes to save man. He
does not feel free, however, to do so, as
an earthly father would do, immediately
upon his child's repentance. He is under the restraint of his own laws, which
must be kept intact to a letter. Some
one must die according to the penalty
prescribed. A substitute may die, and

thus the guilty man go free. The Eternal Son offers himself as a substitute, decends to earth. bodies himself in a man and suffers death. This death is not the eternal death incurred, but the person, being an infinite one, his death is an infinite suffering, and thus its quality makes it equivalent to the quantity of suffering prescribed, and is accepted as a legal discharge of the law in full. Man is therefore released from all claims of the law: divine justice is satisfied. Mercy has room to show itself, and God forgives his child, all in keeping with the mysterious counsel of his own will, and according to his own decree before man was."

"*That you call a consise statement of the plan of salvation as exemplified in the doctrine of the Atonement and Election,*" said Wallace.

"Yes, General, and its beauty, simplicity and reasonableness to a mind divinely prepared for its reception will

give it a standing far above the cold
conclusions of mathematics or logic."

"The orthodox formula," said the
general, "does seem to present the doctrine of Christ's sacrifice as a quit-
claim deed under the law, as in a
commercial transaction. *It means, however, when brought under the searching
scrutiny of the nineteenth century, that
anyone found in the mass of rejected
humanity, whatever saintly virtues he
may possess, despite the Divine decrees,
will find no door open for him to heaven,
— not even a back door,— through which
he might steal while the most High, as
Paul said, ' Winked, though the veriest
brute and beast, who chanced to be one of
the favorite of heaven, might wallow in
the gutter all his days and at death
march straight to the gate of the New
Jerusalem and pass unchallenged in.'*
That's just what this orthodox dogma
of Election and Atonement means, and
meaning this is a revelation made by

the Christian church of the infinite and eternal God, is a blasphemy not easily outdone by the most sacrilegious of infidels. Such dogmas outrage every instinct of humanity, and every principle of justice. It enthrones a veritable monster, a power, whom we can easily enough hate, but whom no one ought to love. It is no wonder, sir, that against the intellectual folly of such blasphemous caricature of the Divine Being the shafts of a scathing satire are hurled, and that against its moral rottenness, the hot bolts of indignation are hurled by the critics of Christianity. There is nothing new or peculiar to Christianity about the orthodox atonement and election. Paul learned it from the ancient Hebrew prophets. It is part of the Mohammedan plan of salvation. The ancient Greeks entertained the same ideas. In the dim distance of Hindu antiquity we see the sages of India discussing the same problems.

" The *principle* underlying the dogma
of the atonement and election, and
which is redeeming in its influence, per-
meates humanity as a whole, and there
are indications of the same law in the
lower orders of life, and it is clearly set
forth in the doctrine of natural selection. Nature selects her races, or individuals, not out of arbitrariness, but
because they are fitted for her purpose.
That purpose is not the happiness of her
favorites, but the progress of the whole.
The races that are fit to survive do
survive, which gives us the scientific
doctrine of the survival of the fittest,
which means the preservation of those
best adapted to carry on the organic
ascent of life still higher. The elect
are not, therefore, the petted favorites
of the Eternal, but His trusted servants.
Almost every individual life is touched
at some point by the mysterious
sweep of this law of sacrifice ; the care
and anxiety, the sleepless nights of a

fond mother for her darling babe; the deep sorrow of father and mother for their erring boy; the agony of the wife or daughter for an intemperate husband or father, *is* vicarious suffering and is redeeming in its influence. The strongest hope of salvation to those low in sin lies in the clinging affection of loved ones, which is daily offering itself a sacrifice for him, and if he is ever saved, he will owe it to the operation of this law of vicarious sacrifice. Every individual salvation is a segment in the sweep of the law under which all salvation out of sin is being wrought."

" But, general, you have several times denounced as unjust the principle that the innocent should suffer for the guilty. Indeed, the chief corner-stone on which rests your opposition to orthodoxy is the very principle of vicarious suffering which you now assert to be universal and wonderfully beneficent.

Will you be kind enough to clear up your logical inconsistencies?"

"I am far from attempting to solve all the mysteries of the almost universal law of sacrificial suffering," said the general. "It does seem a strange and solemn law, but it is not without a holy light breaking out of its shadows. It is not alone the prodigal boy and the intemperate husband and father who are thus saved. Under this law which ordains that the innocent shall suffer with and for the guilty, the father, mother and wife and daughter are also saved. The sacrificial victims have a transfiguration on the altar. The fires of suffering burn out of them the dross of their lower natures. Selfishness, and worldliness, and wickedness, are sublimated into spiritual qualities in the furnace of affliction. Thus the justice and beneficence of nature's method of evolving the higher manhood becomes apparent to human reason. *It is the*

15

arbitrary election and *atonement* of the
Presbyterian. Confession of faith, which
stops at no folly and shrinks from no
blasphemy, whose infamy has no equal
in remorseless logic, that I have denounced. The Westminster Confession
of Faith is the putrification of religion
in dogmas."

"Your philosophy, General." said the
chaplain. "is not a religion; it recog-
nizes nothing but law. Your universe
might as well be without a God. There
are no special manifestations of Divine
power. You have no miracles. Your
philosophy necessitates the rejection of
the miracles in the lives of Joshua, of
Moses and of Job. How can there be
an answer to prayer if there is no over-
ruling providence, no personal super-
vision of our lives and actions? and
how can sins be forgiven?"

"Mr. Chaplain, if your analysis of my
philosophy finds no God, either I have
failed to make myself clear or your

power of analysis is defective. *God is the soul of all that is.* He is everywhere and in everything. Most emphatically and under all circumstances, 'in Him we live and move and have our being.' I recognize the existence of a 'Positive Unknown,' and with Herbert Spencer, speculate that that incomprehensible power is above personality, and not below it; that *It* is as much above intelligence and will as intelligence and will are above mechanical motion. It is true my philosophy does not recognize the possibility of that Power ever forgiving *even one little sin.* There is no domain not governed by law, and the order of nature has never been interfered with, and, judging the future by the past, it will not be. It is asserted by unquestioned authority that "*whatsoever a man soweth, that shall he also reap,*' which, if true, means that sin cannot be forgiven in this nor in any other world. My philosophy authorizes the belief that there may be a relationship established between the devout soul in *secret prayer* and God that gives a comfort unknown to the world. A belief in the alleged miracles in the lives of Job. Joshua and of Moses appears to me to be born of superstition and to be nurtured in ignorance. Scholars now believe Job to have been a mythical character, and the story *of him* to be an allegory. and as such it is both beautiful and helpful. To be able to live a right life in the midst of his surroundings. indicates an exalted manhood. But if the bickering and the final bargain and sale between God and the devil. in view of what Job's former life had been. *is the record of a literal transaction,* then God has reached a plane in moral degradation below that which is occupied by the ruler of the Fiji Islands. and would be a full justification of Mrs. Job when she said, 'Curse God and die.' The alleged

miracles in the life of that brutal mur-
derer, Joshua, are too revolting to be
thought of. In his wars of *invasion* he
murdered men, women and children for
no other crime than defending their
country. The heartless butchery of
'every woman that hath known a man
by lying with him,' and saving alive for
the avowed purpose of prostitution
'thirty-six thousand girls who had not
known a man by lying with him,' has no
equal in the history of brutality and
crime, with the single exception of
David's debauching Uriah's wife, and
then murdering Uriah to conceal his
own infamy, and the most shocking
blasphemy ever offered to Deity is to
charge Him with directing it.

" Moses was one of the most wonderful, and one of the greatest men the
world ever produced. There was nothing in his life, however, that could not
have been done by *a man* wholly without the aid of miracle. During the

twenty years he was absent from Egypt, after having slain the Egyptian, he studied the tides and the passes of the Red Sea. He observed that in the southern part the tide rises nearly sixty feet. He also found a neck of the sea, less than a half mile wide, *that was not under water when the tide was out*, except when the wind was from the south. At this point Napoleon I., his staff, and a part of the one hundred savants taken from France, encamped for the night. An unexpected tide came upon them so suddenly that before their horses were saddled some of them were swimming, and they were only saved from drowning because of Napoleon's command. ' Form a circle around me, and whose horse does not swim we will follow.'

" I have twice ridden through that pass in the Red Sea, and watched the tide as it came in ; a wall of water twenty feet high, and the entire width of the neck of the sea — about a half mile, — rushing on at the rate of a mile in seven minutes, and the reflection that three thousand years ago, Moses and the hosts of Israelites passed through in safety, and that Pharaoh's army was submerged, produced a feeling that all this might have occurred without miraculous intervention and the farther reflection that Moses and Aaron had directed the Israelites to borrow all the valuable jewelry from the Egyptians before starting, and that it was melted and made into a golden calf, and that the calf was subsequently *burned* and the *ashes* scattered, and as the manna which fell from Heaven was nearly as plenty now and just as nutritious, gave to the whole story a very *human* appearance.

"The simple truth is, that Moses, a great leader of men, with the aid of Aaron, took his people out of Egypt to Arabia through the Red Sea when the tide was out, and there was no miracle in it. It was, however, a masterly retreat.

"As a law giver Moses was the equal of Gautama, Buddha and Lycurgus, but was vastly the superior of either of them in generalship. The Ten Commandments were given to the world in almost the same language by Gautama after Moses lived, but there is no evidence that Gautama had any knowledge of their having been written. They were evolved by both of them as they would have been by any other great thinker, as the code for the government of their people.

"Whether Moses visited oriental countries, and while there acquired great dexterity as a 'sleight of hand performer,' will never be known. There is no doubt that he used questionable methods to impress his people with his superiority over them. Such deception was then justified. Even Alexander the Great, several hundred years later, *impressed the soldiers from Greece* that he was the son of the God, Jupiter. His mother was not superstitious, and she often said, with a smile, 'I wish Alexander would cease embroiling me with the gods.'

"He adopted the same adroit method in explanation of the total eclipse of the moon, the night before the battle of the Granicus. He directed the soothsayers and astrologers to say, 'The moon is Darius' friend and the sun Alexander's, and the eclipse of the moon means Darius' defeat to-morrow,' and it did.

"Whether Moses believed his code of law to have been the best that could be, as did the great Spartan law giver, and go into voluntary exile, as did Lycurgus, will ever remain as great a mystery as did the place of their death and burial.

"Moses was a star of the first magnitude in that magnificent constellation of the world's greatest men whose luster is undimmed by time, and any effort made through superstition or ignorance, to rob him of the glory that belongs to him, by alleging miraculous aid, will, in the near future, be removed by a rational interpretation of all the acts of his life."

"Do you, General, leave out of your philosophy the sacrament of the Lord's Supper, baptism and the resurrection of Jesus?"

"Yes, in a literal sense, I do. A disbelief in the efficacy of the Lord's Supper, except as a memorial service, in which sense with the supernatural wholly eliminated, it ·is both beautiful and helpful, and in baptism and the resurrection of the body of Jesus, is no more evidence of disloyalty to His teaching than is the non-participation in a Fourth of July celebration by an American citizen evidence of treason.

"'Truly the letter killeth.' It is not unscientific to believe that a *similarity of feeling* between the human soul and God may be established in secret prayer. If it is true that God breathed into man the breath of life, and that he did is not ques-

tioned, even by scientists, not, however,
by a special creation, but by evolution,
then it is also true that man possesses
something in common with Deity. A
large per cent of scientific men believe
there exists a serial order of ethers, inter-
vening between the atmosphere at one extremity and terminating at the other
extremity, in an ether of infinite attenu-
ation and elasticity, not affected in any
way by the law of inertia. Light is
transmitted with great velocity on an
ether believed to fill all inter-planetary
spaces. The wave lengths of the different colors have been measured. So
mathematical is our knowledge upon this
question that scientists have produced a
dark spot on a screen on which two intensely bright lights were thrown, because the crest of the waves of one
light corresponded with the troughs of
the other light. The same principle can
be demonstrated in sound, by taking two
tuning-forks, one having fifty vibrations

to the minute and the other fifty and a
half; when the crest of the waves from
one corresponds with the trough of the
other silence is the result, after which
the sounds rise again. If the ethereal
undulations that are recognized as light
fall upon the retina of a person at different times, or upon the retina of two
or more persons, however remote they
may be from each other, the *same* sensations are produced; that is, they have a
similarity of feeling so far as the effect
of light is a cause of sensations, if the
ethereal vibrations have the same wave
length and the same number of vibrations to the inch. All light was originally projected from the sun, and all
terrestrial lights are merely temporary
manifestations of that which came from
the primal source in the far-past ages.
All thought was originally projected from
the mind of God, and all terrestrial manifestations of the force called mind are
temporary uses of the ether on which the

primal undulations were initiated, and
upon which all thought is transmitted.
It is as reasonable to believe there is an
ether for the transmission of thought as
there is a "luminiferous ether" for the
transmission of light. The only evidence
of the existence of either is the incon-
cievability of an effect remote from its
cause without a *medium of transmission.*
The velocity of thought has not been
measured as light has been, for the probable reason that its velocity is much
greater, and whether the law of inverse
squares affects its ethereal undulations
has not yet been determined.

"The human soul possessing *a something*
in common with its author, God, may be
put into such a condition of *receptivity*
by *solitude, meditation* and *prayer* that
the ethereal undulations on which thought
is projected may have the same wave
length, and the same number to the inch,
in the human soul as when they emanated
from the mind of God. A similarity of

feeling is thereby established, and the man can love what God loves, upon a scientific basis.

"There is not enough emphasis placed upon the *life* of Jesus, and there is too much upon his death. Every belief in the supernatural touching the birth, life and death of the purest, and the greatest man, Jesus, is an irrational dogma, and will be in the not remote future laid quietly away in the graveyard of forgetfulness, and the pall-bearers on that occasion will be *Unitarian ministers*. The purifying influence of a baptism with the Holy Spirit,— with or without water is a matter of no consequence,— which no forms or ceremonies can limit and no sectarianism can narrow to a favored few, puts all into the warm and genial sunshine of the right life, and leaves them in harmony with God."

CHAPTER XII.

Early in the morning of the 15th of December, 1864. in the midst of a dense fog, the long roll was sounded. A line of battle was formed, and was advanced during the day about two miles. No general engagement occurred that day. Wallace's command captured three or four batteries situated on " Little Round Tops," which are low elevations, having somewhat the appearance of the largest mounds built by the Mound-Builders. About 3 o'clock in the afternoon the right of our line was pushed forward to secure an elevated position on which a battery could be planted to enfilade the Confederate line. The desired position was then occupied by a Confederate battery, which had to be taken. It was supported by infantry of unknown num-

231

ber. Colonel Dale requested the privilege and pleasure of taking General Wallace's old brigade and capturing it. General Wallace reluctantly consented. The brigade took its position ready for the charge. The signal for the charge was the discharge of all the pieces in the battery. A volley from every gun came and every man sprang forward. Their progress was so rapid that although the battery was six hundred yards distant the gunners had time to load but once. That volley was fired at the range of less than twenty rods, with deadly effect. Colonel Dale's horse was torn almost in pieces by a solid shot that struck him in the breast. The colonel sprang to his feet, and was the first man at the battery. As he sprang upon the works and shouted "Surrender!" a thrust was made at his breast with a bayonet in the hands of a Confederate major, but it never reached its mark. A captain seeing the blow, crushed his head with

his musket.   The battery and a thousand
prisoners were taken.   Colonel Dale was
complimented by General Thomas in
person, with the remark :   " That smile
of yours means victory."   Night came
and both armies rested on their arms.

  " Well, Colonel Dale, every movement
to-day has been satisfactory," said General Wallace.   " Our line has advanced
its entire length, and we are now not
to exceed half a mile from the Confederate line, which is about two miles long.
Our loss has been slight to-day, but we
can't hope for so little to-morrow.   The
whole Confederate line has strong breast-
works ; a part of the left of their line is
a stone fence.   It is our present intention to push our line slowly forward to-
morrow morning, and the final charge
will not be made until in the afternoon.
We shall have to charge good works, as
they did at Franklin, and I fear our loss
will be heavy.   I believe a decisive victory in this battle means an end of the

16

war in the West. We diminished Hood's
fighting force about one-third in the
battle of Franklin, and an utter rout
now will be equivalent to a disorganiza-
tion of his remaining force."

"General Wallace," said Colonel Dale,
"I am delighted to hear you say that! I
had speculated a little along that line
myself, and to know that *you* believe it
gives me great hope. I am so glad of
it. While I have been brevetted for gallantry in battle,and complimented enough
to turn my head, I am not a soldier from
choice. I have no love for the roar of
musketry and the wild excitement of
the charge in battle. I cry and pray
every night for the end of the war.
I could have more pleasure in one day
in a quiet home in the North than all the
honor and glory has given in the last four
years. I shall do my duty to-morrow
in the hope it may be the last bloodshed
I shall ever be compelled to see on the
battle-field.

"Yes, Colonel Dale, I know you will do your duty. You never fail, but I wish to caution you against needless exposure. That bayonet thrust to-day was aimed at your heart, and you would have fallen dead just as you sprang on the breast-works, even before the battery was taken, if that captain, in an almost miraculous manner, had not brained your assailant with his gun. I brevetted him brigadier-general, and he is now the happiest man in the army. It was a big jump from captain to general, but he merited the promotion."

"Was the promotion," said Colonel Dale, with a twinkle in his eye, "because he saved my life?"

"Well, the order did not read that way; it said for gallantry in capturing a Confederate battery."

"But, General, I have seen you several times take greater chances of being killed than I ever did. It is your own example I have been following."

"Perhaps that is true, but my case is different from yours. I have nothing to live for. I have not, as you know, made a confidant of any man in the army. I have not distressed even you, my dearest friend, with my sometimes almost unbearable unhappiness. I have been, and am, indifferent to life. Even you do not know that there has not been one night since the death of my poor, dear Agnes that my eyes have not been wet with tears. I think of her the last thought before I sleep, and the first thought when I wake."

The colonel buried his face in his handkerchief, and sobbed aloud: "O, General, I think I know how your heart aches; I pity you, and I pray God that these dark clouds may soon be removed, and be followed by sunshine."

After a long silence, Wallace said: "I have no premonition of evil to either of us to-morrow. We know, however, what there is to be done. If the Con-

federate army remains behind good
works, as it no doubt will, I have no idea
that Hood will leave his position until
he is driven from it at the point of the
bayonet. We must have a victory or
die, both of us. As something may
happen to me I have thought it proper
to prepare this document, which you
will put in some safe place; it is my
will. You are a poor boy. I am amply
able to provide for you, even if you are
disabled so you cannot labor when you
are out of the army; if I am not killed
you may hand it back to me." The
colonel took the paper with trembling
hand, but made no reply. General Wallace looked at his watch and said: "I t
is 12 o'clock. We will retire; good
night."

Picket firing continued during the
whole night, and several times became
so active that a general engagement appeared to be imminent. Morning came
at last, and our line of battle was slowly

pushed forward during the day, and by
3 o'clock in the afternoon the lines of
battle were nearly parallel with each
other, and were about a thousand yards
apart. The Confederate line of battle
terminated on its left abruptly without
a flank, on a hill of considerable eleva-
tion. The right of our line had been
pushed forward so far that two of our
batteries almost exactly enfiladed their
line. Six of our batteries were so situated that they bore directly upon the
Confederate battery situated on the
summit of the hill referred to. Our line
of battle was ready to advance. Orders
had been given that at the cessation of
fifteen minutes cannonading by all the
batteries, the charge was to begin. The
firing was to be as rapid as possible, and
to be directed at the battery on the hill.
Six batteries of six guns each opened at
once. The two batteries on our extreme
right, which enfiladed the Confederate
line, and the four other batteries in their

front was more than any battery could withstand. Their guns were silenced almost at once, and every gun was found an hour later disabled. The crash and the roar was deafening. I had heard a few times before the roar of musketry that was continuous for a few minutes, but I never before that time heard the thunder of artillery that was so near continuous. The sight I shall never forget. With the aid of a glass both lines could be distinctly seen as they stretched away to the left, and with the naked eye all that was in our front.

General Thomas sat quietly on his horse about fifty rods in the rear of our line of battle. General Wallace and Colonel Dale rode back and forth in the rear of Wallace's command. The whole line had been informed, and every man understood, that at the cessation of firing by the batteries the charge was to begin. The firing ceases; the soldiers spring to their feet; General Wallace and Colonel

Dale, with swords drawn, dash along the line. There is new life everywhere. The line is strengthened at the center, directly in front of two Confederate batteries, just now put into position on the dead run: all is ready: a line of battle two and a half miles long, moves forward with the precision and grandeur of a charge by Napoleon's Old Guard. It was like the stately sweep of a gigantic pendulum. The colors flying; the bands and drum corps at regular distances along the line playing "Yankee Doodle." The stretcher corps, of two from each company, was in its place in the rear of the advancing lines of battle. The Confederate line of works in plain view less than half a mile away; every soldier impatiently awaiting the shock: the Confederate batteries on the hill at the extreme left of their line were silent as a grave, but the other batteries along the line were pouring forth volley after volley of shot and shell, presented a view of a battle not before seen during the war, except at Gettysburg.

General Wallace was by nature a soldier, and a leader of men. He watched with evident delight the advancing army. He said to Colonel Dale: "Your persistent smile is evidence that the grandeur of this battle has not escaped you. Why, if the Duke of Wellington were here he would say as he did in one of the charges at Waterloo, "That's splendid."

"Yes, General, the element of grandeur is apparent, but to me the scene is awful as well; and that smile,— if it is a smile,— is only on my face; it does not extend to my heart."

"Colonel Dale!"shouted General Wallace, in a stern voice, a short time after. "Hold that brigade in the center, steady. Push them a little faster. Ah, its all right; they have struck the double-quick; the Confederate skirmish line is falling back; we will have the first volley from their infantry as soon as their skirmishers are inside their works."

Colonel Dale urges his horse down the line to the left to the brigade in the center, and upon which the heaviest artillery was bearing. The whole line is now within four hundred yards of their breastworks: it is sweeping forward in majesty and power. The impetuosity of the charge appears irresistible. The first volley from their infantry is rained upon our line at the range of less than four hundred yards with deadly effect. A dull thud as of tearing strong cloth is heard: a stream of blood gushes from General Wallace's left breast; his sword falls from his hand; he reels in his saddle, and falls to the ground. *General Wallace is dead!* went along the line as if by electricity. General Dale from the moment of Wallace's death, exhibited the rage of personal anger and deep hatred. The tears streaming from his eyes, and his voice

trembling with emotion he rode the line
shouting, "*Avenge the death of Wallace!*" The first volley from their infantry thinned our ranks, but did not
even check our progress. The line never
wavered. On it went as irresistible as
a cyclone! General Dale appeared to
be omnipresent. The smile had disappeared from his face, and in its stead
was an expression of malice and revenge.
The whole line is sweeping forward.
They are now within ten rods of their
line. They have had just time to reload,
and another volley from their infantry,
and of grape and canister from the two
batteries bearing upon the center of the
line, was poured upon them with more
deadly effect than the first. General
Wallace's old regiment held the center,
and was directly in front of the two
batteries, and the strongest part of the
Confederate infantry line.

General Dale at the moment of the
discharge from the batteries and the in-

fantry was in the center of the regiment,
and his horse's head was in advance of
the line; his eye flashing fire and his
stentorian voice thundering: *"Avenge
the death of Wallace!"* His horse is
riddled with minie balls, and grape and
canister pass through its body. In his fall
the general's foot remains in the stirrup,
and underneath the horse's body. By
a superhuman effort he extricates himself, bounds to his feet, and is the first
man to leap upon the works and command. "Surrender!" Immediately after
their last volley, and before the shock
came upon them, the Confederate soldiers, by the hundred, had cut their
cartridge box belts and threw down
their guns in their haste to retreat, and
had fled. A hand-to-hand conflict with
those who remained, in which General
Dale took an active and dangerous part,
followed, and in a few minutes resulted
in a complete victory all along the line.
All who were not killed or captured fled

in every direction in utter rout and
confusion. Hood was disheartened, his
army discouraged, and never existed
again as an army. General Wallace's
regiment lost in killed on the field
more than one-third of its number.

Near where General Dale's horse fell
seven dead soldiers from an Iowa regiment were lying; their bodies were
touching or their limbs overlapping each
other. As soon as Hood's forces were
completely routed, and the decisive victory was won, General Dale directed an
orderly to send him an ambulance at
once. A colonel who was standing near
supposing he was wounded, saluted him
and said : "General, can I do anything
for you — are you wounded?"

"No, Colonel, I thank you. I am not
hurt. Something struck me a heavy
blow in the breast as I approached the
breastworks, and I yet feel a little
pain, but I shall be all right in a few.
minutes."

"Why. General. there is a bullet hole in your coat. over your heart. Let us investigate it."

The coat was unbuttoned and no bullet hole was found through the lining.

"Ah," said the general. "I think I understand it." He put his hand in his breast pocket and brought out a deck of cards, in which a minie ball was sticking. The bullet had passed through every card but one.

The general's voice trembled as he said, "General Wallace and I have spent many pleasant evenings with that deck of cards and it has now saved my life."

Then he sprang into the ambulance and directed the driver to take him to the headquarters wagon, get his trunk, and then to a hotel in the city.

He said to the driver as he entered the hotel: "Wait for me, I will return in a few moments." In ten minutes a tidily dressed young lady appeared and said, "Take me to the hospital where General Wallace is."

"I can't do it. Miss. I am waiting for General Dale, said the driver, "and I dare not disobey orders."

"I assure you it will be all right, the general wishes you to do so."

"All right, Miss, jump in."

A few moments later a young lady entered the hospital and asked for the surgeon.

When he came to her she said, "Is General Wallace dead?" and burst out crying.

"No, Madam," said the surgeon, "he is not dead, and since I have examined the wound more carefully, I am hopeful that he may recover."

"Can I see him?" said she.

"That depends. If you are a southern lady, here out of curiosity to see a fine looking, dashing Union general badly wounded, no, — emphatically no."

She shook her head, the tears still streaming from her eyes.

"Are you a relative or a friend?"

"Yes, Doctor, I was acquainted with the general before he entered the army. He was a dear friend."

"Come with me, Miss, your presence may do him good. He is in our private room, away from the noise inseparable from any army hospital after a great battle."

The surgeon opened the door noiselessly, and entered, followed by the young lady. "General Wallace," said he, "here is a young lady who wishes to see you, and I have granted her the privilege."

The general was looking out of the window toward the battle-field, counting the ambulances as they came loaded with wounded, and he said to himself, as he slowly and indifferently turned his head on the pillow, as if the presence of a young lady at that time was of no consequence :

"That is seventy-five since I began to count." But when he saw her a tremor came over him; he closed his eyes for a minute, and when he opened them again, and she was still standing by his side, he exclaimed:

"Oh, Agnes! Agnes! I knew you would be the first to meet me in heaven; death had no terrors for me. When did I die?"

She gave him her hand and knelt beside the bed, looked calmly into his face and said tenderly, "Donald, you are not dead."

"Not dead," said he, "why you are Agnes?"

"Yes."

"And you have been in heaven four years. Agnes was drowned at sea in a storm. Here is a locket with her picture in it. She sent it to me by Dick Dale, and I have worn it near my heart every minute since. O, Agnes is dead, and we are in heaven."

17

"No, Donald," said she, "putting her hand on his head: "Agnes is not dead. You are in the hospital: you were badly wounded an hour ago. Look at this room *and at the surgeon. This is not heaven.*"

"Am I delirious, or is this only a hallowed dream?"

"You are not delirious," said she, the tears coming into her eyes, "nor is it a hallowed dream, but it *is* a hallowed reality. *Donald, I am your Agnes.* I am here with you in this hospital. Look at this dress, this tie on my neck, this hat and these rings. Did you ever see them before?"

"Yes," said he, "they are what Agnes wore when I stood with her at the gate the night before I enlisted."

"Yes, Donald, you are not mistaken. It is the dress she wore and is wearing now. I have cared more for it than I did for my life, to see if you had forgotten when you last saw it."

He looked her calmly in the face for several minutes, as if bewildered, a smile came over his face, and he said : "O I see it all ; Agnes Murray was not drowned at sea?"

"No," she replied.

"And Dick Dale was Agnes Murray?"

"Yes."

"And you have lived through this four years of bloody war, because you loved me, and wanted to be near me?"

"Yes, Donald."

"Oh, such devotion, such devotion!" He put his right arm around her neck and tenderly drew her face near his own ; he gazed into her tear bedimmed eyes long and lovingly, and then said, as if in prayer, unconscious of the presence of any one : "I thank God for His mercy and goodness to me."

The surgeon beckoned the nurse and they left the room in silence. He said, as he closed the door, and wiped his eyes, "That's no place for me. I am at

home around the amputating table after
a battle or in a hospital, but where soul
touches soul, as is being done in that
room, the scene is too holy to be witnessed, except by angels."

CHAPTER XIII.

A HALLOWED REALITY.

The facts in the case had somehow leaked out. When the surgeon entered the ward from the general's private room, he was met at the door by a score or more, all anxious to know if General Dale was really a girl. Several from his own brigade, who were surprised at his unceremonious departure from the battle-field, thought it possible he might have been wounded.

"Yes," said the surgeon, "strange as it may appear, there is no doubt whatever that General Dale was a girl. She looks to me now as if a mouse would frighten her, notwithstanding the fact that she has fought on many a bloody field, and especially to-day, with the reckless desperation of a demon."

"Yes," said a captain, just back from the battle-field. who was shot through the arm, and had not yet had his wound dressed, "I was in that charge myself, and was near General Dale when the word came that General Wallace was killed. He at once took command of Wallace's old brigade, and while I have been in a good many bloody battles, I never saw anything like it before. It appeared to me he purposely and needlessly rode just where the grape and canister were thickest, and that sentence, 'Avenge the death of Wallace!' Why I hear it yet; it appeared to me to rise above the roar of the battle, *and we did it.* We all loved General Wallace. He would divide whatever he had to eat with any soldier. I have seen him a hundred times walk through the mud half knee deep and let a private soldier ride his horse. At the time of the first volley from the infantry, and of grape and canister from their batteries, when

General Dale's horse was torn to pieces,
it seemed to me nothing could live in
front of their line. I expected to see
him fall pierced with a hundred bullets,
and I do not believe he was a girl."

"Well, Captain," said the surgeon,
"it does appear like fiction, but facts
are sometimes stranger than fiction, and
this is one of *those* facts. It is absolutely true that there has never been the
slightest suspicion during his entire army
life that he was a girl; neither as orderly, major, colonel nor general. He
was not a day sick; he had received no
wound, and he had not been even social
with any one except General Wallace,
on whose staff he had been for more than
two years."

A soldier from an Iowa regiment, who
has since filled places of honor and trust
in the state, said: "I always suspected
he was a girl, his hand was so little and
plump, and he never did get a pair of
shoes small enough for him, and that

funny smile of his, always the most smiling in the greatest danger, was awfully girlish, and don't you forget it."

Another said: "I saw him at Stone River just after his horse was shot from under him, and I am dead sure his moustache was gone, and Bill Levelhead told me not twenty minutes ago that he saw him just after one of the desperate charges at Chickamauga, and that he had no moustache."

Another remembered that when Dick Dale first came to the regiment he did not associate with the other soldiers in any way; that he slept on his blanket in the corner of Major Wallace's tent if it rained, and alone on the outside if it did not rain.

A sergeant pushed his way along the aisle, and with enthusiasm said: "I was standing not ten feet from General Wallace just before the last charge that was made at Resaca. I saw Major Dale ride up to him and say, 'A Confederate

battery has just been hurried into that
timber to our left, and when it opens it
will enfilade our line.' I heard General
Wallace say, 'Take my old regiment out
of the line and capture it.' I saw Major
Dale dash down the line, and I saw the
charge. Oh, it was grand. The battery
fired but one volley before Major Dale
and the regiment were upon it, and
when he rode up to Wallace he had a
nice, black mustauche on, and I also
know when he rode back, saluted the
general, and said, ' We got them,' he had
no moustache.''

At this time General Thomas entered
the hospital and asked the surgeon if it
was proper for him to see General Wallace.

"Certainly," said the surgeon, "come
this way, General."

" Is he mortally wounded? ".

" Not necessarily so, General. His
wound is a dangerous one, but in view
of his good constitution and his nerve,

I have hope of his recovery. His wound is not so serious as was at first thought. The bullet must have grazed the apex of the right lung, but upon a more careful examination, I do not believe the lung was injured. There has not been up to this time any expectoration of blood."

General Thomas grasped Wallace's hand affectionately, and said : "It gives me more pleasure than I can express in words to be able to take your hand, and I have learned from the surgeon that, though your wound is a serious one, it is not likely to prove fatal. Of course you have had the news of the battle."

"Only of the victory. I have heard none of the details."

"Some other time, General, when you are stronger, we will talk of the movements. The victory was a great one, and means much for our cause, but it was at fearful cost. We lost heavy in officers and men. The last charge was as magnificent as I have ever witnessed on a battle-field."

The tears rushed into the eyes of General Wallace, and making a heroic effort to conceal the tumult of his feelings, he said : "And I was not there at my post of duty."

General Thomas placed his hand tenderly on his head, and said : "No regrets, my dear boy. While you could not remain to see it finished, history will give you an important position in originating it. We are thankful to God that you are not among the pale faces now lying on the battle-field. General Wallace can you give me any information as to the whereabouts of General Dale?" said the general, with a twinkle in his eye. "He left the battle-field unceremoniously, *and without orders. I want to see him.*

"General Thomas, let me introduce to you Miss Agnes Murray. I think she can give you the desired information."

The general offered his hand. which
she accepted with the same smile he had
seen before, and said : " Miss Murray, I
believe I have not had the reputation of
possessing much emotion, but taking
your hand gives me a pleasure rarely
ever enjoyed by a general commanding
an army, and a joy I shall never forget.
I was myself giving special attention to
the part of the line you commanded after
the supposed death of Wallace. It was
apparent the Confederate generals were
massing their forces in the hope of breaking our center. I was among the first
to learn that Wallace had been shot
from his horse, and not knowing what
the effect would be on his command.
whether a panic or an increased desperation to avenge his death, I rode near
that part of the line, and I saw your
every action. I saw the danger to which
you exposed yourself: it appeared to
me that every shot from both batteries
in your front was directed at *you*. I saw

no hope of your escape, and it is a miracle
that you are living. I said to myself:
'Such unparalleled rashness and desperation is not wholly due to patriotism
and love of victory; it must have a
deeper meaning.' But," continued the
general, " as General Dale has ceased to
exist as an entity, and as I have no authority over Miss Murray, I find no place
for a reprimand, and I suppose Miss
Agnes Murray will soon be transformed
into Mrs. Wallace."

"Yes, General," said Wallace, "just
as soon as a chaplain comes. I see a
court-house across the way — will somebody be kind enough to attend to the
preliminaries?"

"I will do that with pleasure," said
the surgeon. "While my consent should
have been asked, for the general is now
under my care, I will show my approba-
tion in that way."

"Well, Miss Murray, have you ac-
quiesced?"

Yes, General Thomas, I have obeyed the orders of General Wallace implicitly for four years, and I think it would be unsoldierly to disobey him now."

"I can't wait for the chaplain," said General Thomas. "I will give you my congratulations and blessing now," and taking Agnes' hand in his right, and Wallace's in his left, he gently pressed them together, and said earnestly and reverently, "General Wallace, one of your favorite passages in the Bible comes to my mind: 'Be not deceived; God is not mocked: Whatsoever a man soweth, that shall he also reap.' As sure as God's promises will be fulfilled we know what the harvest will be."

"Heaven's richest blessings await you," Wallace replied, with apparent emotion. "Such a compliment, General, from such a source is our first benediction."

CHAPTER XIV.

THE FACTS IN THE CASE.

"It all appears like a dream to me yet," said Wallace, on waking the next morning, "*but it is reality.* Isn't it, Agnes?"

"Yes, Donald," she said, "the past four years has been to me an awful reality. I have, during that whole time lived a life of questionable honor. It has been a false life. I have cried over it, and prayed every night to be forgiven. I ought to have told you everything before we were married."

"While I have known," said Donald, with a smile, "quite a good deal of your life in the past four years, it is not too late to make a confession if you will feel better after having done so."

"Yes, if it is not too late, I want to tell you all, and then ask you to forgive me."

"Until you left me at midnight, the night before you made that speech at the court-house and enlisted, I had never thought of being separated from you. I spent the remainder of the night thinking whether I could live on at home and you in the army. I determined before morning to visit my relations in Scotland, and to confide in my cousin, Minnie, all my plans. I bought in New York the suit of clothes I had on when I came to your regiment. I had a trunk made with a concealed apartment in the bottom, large enough to hold all the clothing I wore. I bought six mustaches. I had my hair cut, leaving it quite long for a boy, and as you know my hair naturally parted on the side, so that I appeared quite boyish, even without the mustache. I bought a ticket for London on the Leota, intending to return to the United States as soon as possible *as a boy*, and join your regiment. My stateroom was next to a young lady from New York, on her way to London, whose acquaintance I made before we left the city. She was of Scottish ancestry and was my own age to a day. I believe she was the happiest person I ever saw. She was engaged to a young man in London, doing business for a rich firm in the United States, of which his father was a partner, and they were to be married on her arrival. We made confidants of each other. She told me of their intended travels. 'We are,' said she, 'going to spend a few months in Paris, and about six months in Italy. O, I am so impatient to get to Rome. I think I shall buy that "classic Tiber" I hear so much about, and bring it home with me.' Her merry ringing laugh almost made me forget myself, and then she continued, 'We are going to Alexandria and up the Nile, and we are going to climb to the *top of the pyramids*.' She put her arms round my neck and kissed

me, and in a playful manner said:
'Aggie, when we are in Alexandria, I
am going to hunt for the remains of the
library that was destroyed by that great
naughty Cæsar, and if I find it I will
bring you a book to remember me by.
We are going to Jerusalem by the way
of the Suez Canal. We expect to spend
six months in the Holy Land, and then
we go to the City of Babylon. I understand the city dads in Babylon have
preserved a few hundred bottles of the
wine left after Alexander the Great's
fatal debauch, and if I find one with the
labels still on I will bring it home. *We
wont hang our harps on the willow trees*,
but we will make them wake up and
take their medicine. Whether we will
visit the land of the droop-eyed, lop-
eared celestials we have not determined,
but we are coming home past the island
of Ceylon, and I'll stop off long enough
to catch a full-grown gorilla,—a six-
footer,—for you. They make the nicest

pets in the world, but you have to keep them chained, or stand over them with a club. Oh, Agnes,' she said very tenderly, and taking me by the hands, 'I do wish you could be as happy as I am.'

" I kept no secret from her, and when I told her how I loved you, and who you were, and that I believed you loved me, but you had never said so, she put her arms around me and sobbed as if her heart would break, and said, 'Oh yes, he loves you, and you will yet be happy with him. The war will soon be over, you and Wallace will marry, and then Charley and I will come and see you.' I took her into my state-room and put on my boy's suit to have her opinion on the disguise. She said, 'That mustache is a stunner. Nobody would think of you being a girl. You look like my brother Dick, and he's a masher.' On the fourth day out from New York, early in the morning, the Leota was disabled in that storm and sunk. I was

up before daylight, and walked the deck
lonely and alone. I saw the first indications of the storm. I had an impres-
sion, and I could not rid myself of it,
that the vessel would be wrecked. I
went to my state-room, changed my
apparel, and put what I now have on
into the concealed apartment in my
trunk. I had, while in New York, put
my hair that had been cut off carefully
in the bottom. I remained in my room
until the wheels were disabled and the
wildest excitement prevailed among the
passengers. I then went on deck as
Dick Dale, and did what I could to
calm the fears of the passengers. I
only heard three references to myself
in the excitement in leaving the vessel
in the lifeboats. The captain said,
'Where is Miss Murray.—I have not
seen her?' Somebody replied, 'She
left ten minutes ago with eleven others
and they all went down before their
boat was twenty feet away.' An el-

derly lady said, 'Where is that young
lady who sang Home, Sweet Home for
us?' Another said, 'She was among
the first to leave the vessel and was
lost.' The first person I met on the
deck was Miss Marion Summers; she
was wild with fear, but was asking
everyone if they had seen Agnes Murray. I stood near her and looked in
her face to see if she would recognize
me, and said, 'Is she in her room?'
'Oh, no,' she cried, 'she is not there.'
She hurried into a lifeboat; it was in a
few moments capsized, and I saw her
last struggles. The captain, the mate
and I were the last to leave the sinking
vessel in the least seaworthy of all the
lifeboats. In six hours we were picked
up by a steamer bound for New York.
I took the train at once for your regiment. My sex was not discovered for
several reasons. I was not a day sick
while I have been in the army. Your
uniform kindness to me obviated the

necessity of my associating with the soldiers : *for which I can never love you enough*. On the first morning after I came to the regiment I would have told you who I was, for I had concluded during the night to do so, but you said not to tell the secret unless you were mortally wounded. My indifference to life, and my recklessness on the battle-field was because I expected you to be killed, and I wanted to die first. I kept a letter in my coat pocket, directed to you, giving you the facts and who I was, with the request that my body be taken to you if I was killed. I never purposely exposed myself to danger in the hope of being killed until yesterday. When the word came along the line, ' General Wallace is killed,' I determined to die in the last charge. I lost, in action, four mustaches. I think you never saw me without one on. I have two yet. How do I look with it on now ? "

" Well, really Agnes, it is not unbe-
coming. You are Dick Dale without a
doubt, but I wont ask you to wear that
name except on special occasions. I am
partial to the name, *Agnes*, you know."

" I thought twice you suspected who
I was, and I would not have hesitated
to tell you, if you had asked me. I was
so tired of battle. Donald, can you forgive me ? "

"Come and sit on the bed near me,"
said he, "and put your hand in mine.
Why it *is* as soft and plump as a girl's,
isn't it ? Agnes, I am one of the most
forgiving of mortals, and I solemnly
pronounce your sins absolved. I trust
you will never again think of apologizing for any act of a life so near divine
as yours has been."

They are both living at this time, May
1, 1895. They have passed the zenith
of life ; they are looking toward the
setting sun ; it is probably late in the
afternoon of life to both of them. They

have implicit confidence that the incomprehensible aggregation of matter and force that constitutes the " Ego" will defy the laws of matter and force now recognized. and ride the wreck of worlds in an eternal existence; that the sun will rise again on a more beautiful shore. and that their love for each other will endure when the stars melt. Their children are men and women now. and they attest the inexorable law of heredity. "A pure fountain cannot send forth impure waters."